A PROUD TASTE FOR SCARLET AND MINIVER

Written and illustrated by

E. L. KONIGSBURG

Aladdin Paperbacks
New York London Toronto Sydney Singapore

For Manci and for David,
who taught me freedom from its two directions.

First Aladdin Paperbacks edition October 2001

Aladdin Paperbacks
An imprint of Simon & Schuster
Children's Publishing Division
1230 Avenue of the Americas
New York, NY 10020

Also available in an Atheneum Books for Young Readers hardcover edition
Designed by Nancy Gruber
Printed and bound in the United States of America
2 4 6 8 10 9 7 5 3

Library of Congress Catalog Card Number 73-6320
ISBN 0-689-30111-1 (hc.)
ISBN 0-689-84624-X (pbk.)

Contents

Inside
Heaven

DURING HER LIFETIME Eleanor of Aquitaine had not been a patient woman. While she had lived, she had learned to bide her time, but biding one's time is a very different thing from patience. After she had died, and before she had arrived in Heaven, it had been necessary for Eleanor to learn some patience. Heaven wouldn't allow her Up until she had. But there were times, like today, when she wasn't sure whether she had really learned any patience at all or whether she had simply become too tired to be quarrelsome.

Today she was restless. She paced back and forth so rapidly that the swish of her robes ruffled the treetops below. For today was the day when her husband, King Henry II of England, was to be judged. Today she would at last know whether or not—after centuries of waiting—he would join her in Heaven.

Henry had died even before she had. He had died in the year 1189, in July of that year, and Eleanor had spent fifteen years on Earth beyond that. But Eleanor's life had not been perfect; she had done things on Earth for which there had been some Hell to pay, so she had not arrived in Heaven immediately. Finally, the world's poets had pleaded and won her case. Eleanor had been a friend of music and poetry while she had lived, and musicians, artists and poets play an important role in the admissions policies of Heaven; with their pull Eleanor had moved Up. Even so, she had not arrived in Heaven until two centuries after she had died and long after her first husband and some of her best friends had made it. Now it was late in the twentieth century, and Henry still had not moved Up.

Eleanor began drumming her fingers on a nearby cloud.

"You keep that up, and you'll have the Angels to answer to for it," said a voice, one cloud removed.

"Oh, Mother Matilda, I swear you could nag a person to a second death."

A man sitting beside Mother Matilda pleaded, "Your mother-in-law is only reminding you that we have all been requested to stop drumming our fingers and to stop racing back and forth. The Angels don't appreciate having to answer hundreds of requests for better television reception."

"I know, William, I know," Eleanor answered.

"After all," Mother Matilda added, "we are every bit as anxious as you are to know the outcome of today's Judgment."

"You ought to be patient, my lady," William said.

"Yes," Eleanor answered. "I know. I know what I ought to be. I have always known what I ought to be."

But the truth was that Eleanor actually enjoyed not being patient. When she felt impatient, she felt something close to being alive again. Even after more than five hundred years in Heaven, Eleanor of Aquitaine still missed quarreling and dressing up. Eleanor missed strong, sweet smells. Eleanor missed feeling hot and being cold. Eleanor missed Henry. She missed life.

She sighed. She wanted to be there the minute Henry arrived—if he would; there was a great deal to tell him. It had taken Eleanor almost five hundred years to catch up on the two hundred she had missed. She often thought that the worst thing about time spent in Hell is that a person has no way of knowing what is happening on Earth. In Heaven at least, one could watch, even if one could not participate. Only Saints and Angels were allowed to interfere in Earthly affairs. Everyone in Heaven had periods of Earth time about which they knew nothing. Everyone except the Saints; they always came Up immediately following death, and, of course, Heaven had always been home to the Angels. But Saints were hardly the people to contact when you wanted to catch up on the news. Most of them had been more concerned with Heaven than with Earth even during their lifetimes, and now it was almost impossible to move them even a whisper away from the Angels.

Eleanor turned around looking toward the night side of Earth. Perhaps she could spot an outdoor movie screen. Watching that would help her pass some minutes. As she turned her face toward night, and her back toward the two people waiting with her, she spotted Abbot Suger. Eleanor called to him, and the good Abbot stopped to rest at her side.

"Haven't seen you for a long time, Abbot," she said.

"Oh," he answered, "I was over at admissions. They just let an English teacher Up, and he made a beeline for Shakespeare."

"They all do."

"Yes, I know," the Abbot chuckled, "but I like to watch."

"What did this one want to discuss?"

Abbot Suger laughed out loud. "This one didn't want to discuss anything. He presented Mr. Shakespeare with a list of errors he had made in geography and history."

"I wonder how he smuggled his list past the Judges. No one is supposed to carry a single grudge into Heaven, let alone a list of them."

"Oh, I don't know," the Abbot said. "I sometimes suspect that the Judges close an eye. It's always fun to see an English teacher's first encounter with Shakespeare. I think that the Judges, serious as they are, enjoy it, too."

Eleanor said, half to herself, "Shakespeare wrote a play about my son King John that wasn't too accurate either. He gave me a small part in it, but he certainly didn't give me any good lines."

"Ah, Eleanor," Abbot Suger replied, "Shakespeare was far better at writing of heroes than of heroines."

"Maybe so," she said, "but then I wonder why he wrote nothing of Henry."

"Oh! my goodness," Suger said, "he wrote of Henry. Plenty of Henrys. He wrote *Henry IV*, *Henry V*, *Parts I* and *II*, *Henry VI*, *Part I* and *Henry VI*, *Part II*."

"But not my Henry!" Eleanor shouted.

"Eleanor! Eleanor!" Abbott Suger said, "Calm down."

"You never knew my Henry," Eleanor said. "You only knew Louis, my first husband."

"And my foremost pupil," the Abbot added.

"Shakespeare should have written of my Henry." Eleanor poked at the cloud absentmindedly. She continued staring at the cloud and said in a low voice, "Henry is being judged today. That's why I'm so excitable. And that's why they're here," she added, flinging a look over her shoulder. "The lady is Henry's mother, Matilda-Empress, and the man is William the Marshal, a true and loyal knight."

Abbot Suger glanced in the direction that Eleanor indicated and nodded and smiled at the man and the woman. They nodded back. The Abbot then leaned closer to Eleanor and asked, "Who is pleading Henry's case?"

"Lawyers," Eleanor answered. "I always knew that if we ever got enough lawyers into Heaven, they would plead for him."

"Why would lawyers plead for a king? Kings have long been out of fashion with the law."

"My Henry laid the foundation of the whole court system of England," Eleanor announced proudly.

"Really?"

"Henry was due Up long before this, but it had taken almost eight hundred years to get enough lawyers Up to make a case."

"Yes," Abbot Suger agreed, "in Heaven lawyers are as hard to find as bank presidents." Abbot Suger nodded his head, trying to remember something back in the centuries. "Eleanor," he said hesitatingly, "was it not Henry who made you a prisoner?"

"It certainly was," Eleanor agreed. "Henry kept me locked up for fifteen years."

"And you still want him with you in Heaven?"

"Oh, goodness! yes. I think Heaven is much what he deserves. I want him to be every bit as bored as I am . . ." She laughed, looking quickly over at Suger to see if what she had said had made him angry. After all, Abbot Suger was a priest, and priests have always held Heaven in very high regard. But Abbot Suger was not angry; he had a good sense of humor. He had always been a favorite of Eleanor's.

Abbot Suger asked, "Why did you divorce Louis? I was Below when you did; I missed it."

"I knew you would not go straight to Heaven. I knew that you were too much in love with the world for an abbot."

"Actually, Eleanor, I have no complaints. Any man with responsibilities in government is bound for Hell, at least for a little while. But I spent less than a century Below. I arrived Up shortly before you died. I looked down on you on your deathbed. You seemed to have died in peace."

"How did you know that Henry had made me a prisoner?"

"Oh, the usual deathbed gossip—accounting good deeds and bad."

"Was my divorce from Louis listed in the good column or the bad?"

"The bad. Why did you divorce him?"

Eleanor tilted her head and smiled. "Because you weren't there any longer to hold us together, I guess. You died, remember?"

"Of course I remember dying. I remember everything. I remember our first meeting in Bordeaux when you were to wed the young Louis, the boy whom I had taught to love God."

"How did Eleanor appear to you when you first saw her?" Matilda-Empress asked, moving forward.

"That is hard to say," Abbot Suger answered.

"Why?"

"Because my first look at her was colored by her reputation. And her wealth."

Matilda-Empress smiled. "I must say that I, too, had an eye on Eleanor's lands before I set eyes on her."

"And I," said William the Marshal, "first encountered Queen Eleanor in defense of her person and her wealth." No one said anything. "As well befitted a man of my calling," William added. Everyone looked at William, but still they said nothing. "I was a knight, you know."

"Yes, we know," said Matilda-Empress.

"Yes," Eleanor added, "a true and noble knight."

Matilda-Empress turned from William and addressed the abbot. "I am curious about the young Eleanor."

"My mother-in-law cannot believe that what I am now is an improvement over what I was then. Tell her what she wants to know, Abbot Suger. Tell her about the young Eleanor. It will help all of us to pass the time."

"Certainly," Abbot Suger said. "It is good to review."

"Ah, Abbot, you, too, miss living. Heaven is often a pale substitute."

Suger spun his head around toward Eleanor; he attempted a frown, but he couldn't manage one. His face broke into a broad grin. "Bite your tongue, lady."

Eleanor laughed. "Certainly, Abbot. Only I speak it, even though we both think it. Now, let us remember. Come, Abbot, Mother Matilda, William, come. Let us remember together."

Part one
Abbot Suger's Tale.

1

KING LOUIS VI and I were staying in a hunting lodge outside Paris when word came that William, Duke of Aquitaine, had died. Just before his death, Duke William had sent messengers to his king; the messengers carried a request. They knew the king would listen, for although the Duke of Aquitaine was a vassal to the king, he was far richer, just as an oilman may be far richer than a prime minister.

William of Aquitaine had a daughter; her name was Eleanor. William's death made Eleanor the richest orphan in Europe. But in those days when all the lords of Aquitaine were fighting among themselves as well as fighting their duke, it took a lot of brawling to hold onto the lands. No woman could do it alone. William knew that his daughter would need a husband, and that is why he had sent messengers to his king. William of Aquitaine wanted his daughter Eleanor wed to the king's son, Prince Louis. With Eleanor would come her lands. With Louis would come a title. A good marriage. A marriage of pomp and pocketbook. William of

Aquitaine knew that King Louis could not pass up a bargain.

And, sick though he was, King Louis VI did not.

The king was ill, very ill. We had left Paris to escape the summer's heat. Louis suffered more than most people from the heat, for he was overweight. History books call him *Louis le Gros*, which means Louis the Fat. He was fat; he could neither put on his own shoes nor mount his horse, but his mind was as lean and as quick as his body was fat and slow. He lost no time in calling the prince to his side and telling him that he was about to be married. Louis was seventeen at the time.

"Yes, father," Young Louis said, "whom do you wish me to marry?"

"The Duchess of Aquitaine," Louis the Fat answered.

"Yes, father," Young Louis replied. He turned and started to leave his father's room. (The smell in the room helped to keep all of the king's interviews short.) Prince Louis had a second thought; he turned back and asked, "Is she old, father?"

"Old enough," Louis the Fat answered.

"Yes, father."

I followed Young Louis out of the castle and began walking with him. We were good friends. He was a head taller than I. Most men were. But Louis was fair, and I was proud of his good looks. I loved everything beautiful, thanks be to God, but I especially loved Louis. I felt like a father to him. In a sense I was his father—his spiritual one. I had been his teacher.

"Her name is Eleanor," I began.

"Oh?" Louis answered, trying to act unconcerned.

"Yes. Her name is Eleanor, and she is well educated."

"Does that mean, dear Abbot, that she embroiders beautifully and knows the proper order in which to hand armor to a knight?"

"Yes, it does." I smiled, "but in this case, fortunately, it also means something more. She can read Latin, and I am told that she knows a great deal of music and poetry. She comes by those talents naturally; her grandfather was a poet as well as a knight."

"Do all these talents occupy a fair head or a plain one?" Louis asked.

"A fair one, I am told."

"An old one?" the prince asked.

"In many ways *old*. She has traveled much and seen much."

Young Louis's hands dropped to his sides. He could act casual no longer. "I may marry the dowry for my father, but I must marry the dame for me. I must know, Abbot. Is she an old lady?"

I laughed. "She is fifteen, Louis. Only fifteen, but

that is the least of her measures. In many ways she is much more than fifteen."

Louis laughed. "Oh, Abbot, I am relieved. I am so inexperienced with women that I do not want someone who is very old." Then he had second thoughts. He turned suddenly and asked, "What do you mean when you say that fifteen is the least of her measures? Is she fat?"

"No," I reassured him. "She is the daughter of a William, not a Louis."

The prince smiled.

King Louis put me in charge of gathering men and materials for our journey to Aquitaine. The king was too sick to do it, but even if he had been well, he would have given the job to me. I had excellent taste, thanks be to God, and a great gift for organizing.

I called together all the important dukes and counts who were vassals of the king, and I fitted them with elegant armor and trappings. I selected a jeweled ring and a gold buckle, worked with enamel, for the prince to give his bride as a wedding gift.

As we rode through the lands that lay between Eleanor and Louis, we paid every toll at every bridge and every tax at every crossing. We carried as many supplies as we could, buying only what we had to. When high prices were asked, we paid them with a smile. We never haggled. I would not allow it. It would not have been dignified.

Even so, the trip was not easy. The armor was elegant, but it was also uncomfortable. It grew hotter because we were moving further into summer and further into the south. At times the glare of the sun striking the armor blinded the men behind. And hot! The men complained that they were being served to Eleanor as a human stew—cooked in their own salt water. I thanked God that I was a simple man of the cloth. But for the sake of the others it became necessary to travel at night.

Finally, we arrived at Bordeaux, the town where the wedding was to take place. We camped across the river from the city and rested; we wanted no trace of weariness to show when we appeared at the palace the next morning.

But Prince Louis was restless, unable to sleep. He came into my tent. "Abbot," he began, "if Eleanor is such a great prize, why was she not engaged long before now? Rich girls are usually betrothed as infants."

"Ah, Louis," I said, "I could ask you the same question. Rich princes also are betrothed as infants."

"But in my case the answer is simple, Abbot. I was not meant to be rich. I am a second son. I was meant to be a priest, and I would have been one if my brother

Philip's horse had not tripped over that old sow and broken Philip's neck in the process. He, not I, was born to be the king of France. I am second son and second choice, and that is why I have not been promised in marriage. What is Eleanor's reason?"

"I think," I said, "that the fair Eleanor was saved because her father and her grandfather thought that they would never die."

"Were they pious men, Abbot?"

"Eleanor's grandfather, William the Troubadour, went on Crusade to the Holy Land."

"That does not answer my question. Bored men, fortune hunters, and second sons also go on Crusades. Their reasons are not always religious."

"Let me explain it with an example. I once heard Eleanor's father, Duke William, at prayer."

"Did he appear serious?"

"Serious? Oh, yes, quite serious."

"And sincere?"

"Sincere? If you mean by that that he believed what he was saying, I have to call him sincere."

"Serious and sincere. What more can you ask of a man in prayer, Abbot?"

"Humility."

"Was the duke not humble?"

"You judge," I answered. "The duke got down on one knee. He clenched his fist and poked it into the sky.

'Dear Lord,' he began, 'this is William, Duke of Aquitaine, speaking. You may have heard from Count Raymond already, but I am telling you to let his prayers go unanswered, for he is a liar, O God. I give You my word and my hand, God. Put Your strength into my fist, O God, and together we shall teach Count Raymond a lesson. And then after, dear God, I'm going to make a nice donation to one of Your churches.' Duke William then lowered his arm and marched into battle convinced that the power of God was on his side, his right side; he was right-handed. He defeated Raymond, by the way."

Young Louis looked astonished. "I have never before heard anyone regard a prayer as a challenge match between himself and God. Let us hope that there is something more of her mother than of her father in Eleanor."

"Whatever there is of her mother would have been planted but not cultivated. Her mother, may she rest in peace, died when Eleanor was still very young."

The prince mumbled good night and went to his tent. His tent was beautiful—blue, decorated with the lilies of France. I had designed it. Thanks be to God, the design had turned out well.

Eleanor wore a dress of scarlet, of a cloth so fine that it looked as if it had been woven by the wind. The hem had a delicate pattern of silver threads. The color set off her gray eyes and fine features. Yes, Eleanor was beautiful. A beauty that is bred as much as it is born. She was lively and witty and completely without pretenses or patience. It was she who greeted us at the castle door. She had not yet learned to wait.

As our party of knights and nobles entered the castle door, she asked, "Which of you is Louis?"

The prince stepped forward and bowed. Thank goodness, good manners did not require him to say anything at that point, for Louis appeared to be struck dumb.

Eleanor curtsied. *Her* tongue was not tied. "Louis Capet," she said as she looked at her husband-to-be from the tip of his head to his spurs, "I hope that you are as convinced as I that we both could have done worse. Much worse."

And that was the first thing that Eleanor said that Louis would not have an answer for.

2

THE WEDDING took place two weeks later, a short engagement. It would have been shorter if it had not taken that long to gather Eleanor's vassals from the far corners of her lands. During those two weeks I spent my time studying the churches of Bordeaux. I had in mind rebuilding my church at St. Denis, and with God's help I was searching for a new way to make buildings higher and let in more light. The old churches of Bordeaux were built in a heavy style. I didn't want my church dumped onto a foundation. I wanted it to soar above it.

Young Louis was overwhelmed by his good fortune. Each night he would come to me and tell me something new he had discovered in this amazing Eleanor.

"Do you know, dear Abbot, that she has the liveliest mind!"

"Yes, my prince."

"And style. She has that, she has style. A style all her own."

"Yes, my prince."

"And wit. I have never known anyone who could turn a phrase so."

"Yes, my prince."

"She is an excellent horsewoman. I can barely keep up with her."

"Louis, my prince, you are putting yourself on the light side of the balance in everything but piety."

"And good fortune, dear Abbot. I am betrothed to the fairest lady in all of Europe, and she is betrothed to a poor second son, one that fortune has raised to be heir to the king of France and husband to a great lady."

Eleanor and Louis were married first in Bordeaux. They then traveled to Poitiers and were married again. Eleanor arranged both weddings. She arranged everything. She was not shy about making decisions, about giving orders, about receiving homage or receiving gifts. Eleanor was as much at ease arranging a ceremony as she was arranging her dress. She knew what she wanted, and she had the energy to do it all. Indecisiveness wears a person out. Eleanor was never weary.

After the second ceremony, Eleanor and Louis chose to vacation in Poitiers before traveling north to meet Louis's father, the king.

Louis appeared at chapel one morning wearing the crown of the Duke of Aquitaine. "Ah, Abbot," he said,

Eleanor of Aquitaine
married Louis of France
in Bordeaux on July 25,
1137

"three of our barons have yet to come to pay me homage. Foolish men! They will soon learn that I am now their overlord. I am to be listened to. I will be listened to. I will not only be listened to, I will be heard. I am the Duke of Aquitaine, the prince and heir of the Kingdom of France. I am vassal to no one . . ."

"Except to God," I interrupted. "Louis, please, take off that crown. You are in His house; He is the King of Kings."

Louis whipped the crown off his head, held it over his chest and bowed. Then he said his morning prayers.

While we were waiting for the barons and lords to come to Poitou and pay their respects (and their wedding gifts) to Louis and Eleanor, messengers arrived from Paris. We were at dinner at the time, Eleanor and Louis at the center of the head table; I was at Louis's right. The meals were long, each course followed by acts of jugglers and troubadours. Eleanor needed troubadours as much as she needed food; there was much merriment and confusion, so the appearance of the messengers created no special stir. Their message did. King Louis the Fat had died.

I rose from my place at the table and walked around it until I stood in front of Eleanor and Louis. With only the table between us, I bowed. "My king," I said, kneeling to Louis. "My queen," I said, bowing my head in the direction of Eleanor. They understood. Louis's reaction was quiet, private; Eleanor's, quick, public.

"Announce the death of my good father-in-law to our subjects who are gathered here," she said. "Tell them that they came to dine with a duchess and find they have supped with a queen."

And thus ended our stay in Poitiers.

When Eleanor arrived in Paris, she arrived as bride, Duchess of Aquitaine, and as Queen of France.

3

FROM HEAVEN I can look down on Paris and know why it is called the City of Light. It sparkles with lights and flowers. In the twelfth century Paris was not called that, and yet it was even then a city of light—the light of knowledge. As towns went, Paris was actually very small and rather dingy and cold compared to the cities we had just visited in the South. But it was still an exciting place to be. It was a city of ideas, the place where everyone came to study; it was the city of the University. Students took lodgings in places along the Left Bank, and it is amusing to hear that part of Paris still being called the Latin Quarter because eight hundred years ago, students from all over Europe met there and communicated with each other in a common tongue —Latin.

Eleanor and Louis were crowned together at Christmas. King Louis and Queen Eleanor of France. Louis had been crowned once before when his brother Philip had died; he was only ten then and had been brought blinking from the monastery where he had been studying. King Louis the Fat had his son crowned during his lifetime so that no one could fight over the succession when he died. With disease and fire and war as constant enemies, kings as well as dukes lived close to sudden death.

They chose to hold the ceremony in Bourges, a city that was close to the borders of both their lands. The coronation was as colorful and lively as Eleanor could arrange. I offered a few suggestions, too, and, thanks be to God, those parts I recommended turned out beautifully.

It was a day several years later as I was working on some designs for some stained glass for my new church at St. Denis, that I received a visit from Adelaide, Louis's mother and (alas!) Eleanor's mother-in-law.

"I am leaving Paris," she said.

"Really?"

"Yes," she answered, "Eleanor has crowded me out."

"Surely, my lady, there is room in a castle for two queens."

"If one of them is Eleanor of Aquitaine, there is not room enough in all of Paris for two queens," Adelaide replied. I did not answer. Adelaide went on, "There is no place for me in my son's life. There was hardly room for me at the coronation ceremony. And now she has crowded me out of my castle."

"How so, madam?" I asked.

"She has imported from her lands troubadours and flutists. Men who play the tambourines and some who play the viol. They follow her around and make noise. When I ask Eleanor how she can live with such confusion, she answers that from their flutes blow the warm winds of the South. Otherwise, she finds Paris gray and chilly. Besides, Abbot, she spends money too easily, too lavishly. It is not Christian to desire such riches—she buys costly silks and imported spices and burns incense because she says the palace stinks. Isn't that an ugly word, Abbot? *Stinks!*"

I smiled. "An ugly word best suits an ugly quality."

"And she wears cosmetics! Is it not wrong to paint one's face and dress up. Abbot Bernard cautions against such display, such finery."

"My dear Adelaide," I answered, "there are those who believe that only by seeing beautiful things, only by surrounding ourselves with beautiful things can we understand the absolute beauty, which is God."

"You may believe that, Abbot Suger, but I don't." Adelaide paused, squinted her eyes and continued, "Can you tell me why my daughter-in-law should choose to crowd me out of my own bedchamber?"

"How did she do that, my lady?"

"With tapestries. She covered all the walls of my bedchamber with tapestries that she had ordered to be woven for the purpose. They are hunting scenes from her homeland. How can a person rest in a room that is hung with men's eyes that look down on one wherever one turns. And those parts that have no eyes are full of gore. Blood and guts of animals. Eleanor says that the red brightens the room and that the tapestries themselves keep out the damp."

"She is right, my lady. A castle can be a drab place. I am rather fond of tapestries and color myself."

"I tell you, Abbot, I am leaving."

"Why do you not simply remove the tapestries, madam?"

"I have. I have twice ordered them taken down. And both times they have been put back up. If I leave the castle to attend church, she uses that time to have the tapestries rehung. If I take a short ride, the tapestries are rehung. I ask you, Abbot, am I to stay in my chamber to guard its walls?"

"And what does your son, the king, say?"

"Nothing. He says nothing. He smiles. He admires her determination. I tell you, Abbot, she has him bewitched. He is no longer the sweet boy we reared. When I asked him if he would like to wake in the morning and look upon the blood and gore of tapestries, he said, 'No, Mother, I much prefer to wake in the morning and look upon Eleanor.' "

I could not help but smile. "I would offer to help, but the king will not listen to me either. He listens only to

Eleanor. It is a stage he must go through. Eleanor is too much woman. Right now, she is young and ambitious. She needs some years, some maturity."

"She needs a child," Adelaide said. "She needs to give us an heir. Poor Louis could be killed at any moment, what with all the wars he has to wage to keep peace in her lands."

"They are also now Louis's lands. He cannot have those lands without Eleanor, and further, he cannot hold them without war."

"True, my dear Suger, but you admit that she has made him less than kind in his treatment of conquered people. Remember last year when he ordered his knights to cut the hands off every man in Poitiers, and he took all the women and children as hostages. It would have been a shame on all the Capets if you had not gone to Poitiers and talked him out of that."

"Yes, it would," I admitted. "Louis has been unnecessarily harsh with some people, but, thanks be to God, I understand the situation. Only a man who is certain of himself can afford to be generous to his enemies. Louis is still trying to prove to Eleanor that he is a man. He goes about it the wrong way. He tries to be her kind of man, and neither of them is sure what that is. He listens to her instead of to his conscience. Eleanor is not a woman who can respect a man she is able to order around. I do not offer my counsel anymore. If I were to give in to her whims, I would lose both her respect and a pure conscience. In time Louis will learn the same."

"She knows nothing of kindness, that daughter-in-law of mine."

"Eleanor is kind, basically kind, but she knows nothing of fair play; she needs to learn about justice. And in time she will. When she does, your daughter-in-law will be a great queen."

Adelaide was not convinced. "The only thing great about her is her nerve. She has got my poor Louis involved in a terrible war with the Duke of Champagne, after my dear husband, may God rest his fat soul, worked so hard to establish peace with him. Trouble seems to be the only kind of excitement Eleanor understands. I tell you, Abbot, I am leaving Paris. My counsel is no longer needed, and neither is yours. We are both out of jobs."

"Not I," I answered. "I always have work. I am rebuilding my church. Thanks be to God, I have a brilliant new idea. My structure will be very high, and it will allow tall windows, colored windows like jewels. Its style will be very modern. You must come to the dedication of my rebuilt church."

"It is well, dear Abbot Suger, that you have so many

interests. I know of nothing I want to be besides wife of one king and mother to another. God has taken my first job from me, and the Devil has taken the second."

"Are you choosing to leave your son to the Devil?"

"Yes. The She-Devil, Eleanor. But Louis will need you again, Abbot. Promise me that when he does ask for your help, that you will answer his call."

"Oh, most happily, dear Adelaide. Thanks be to God, I enjoy affairs of state as much as anything."

Queen Adelaide left Paris and married again. She was too old to become a mother again, but she rescued the other half of her talents, that of being a nagging wife.

4

THE WARS with Champagne continued, and Louis grew bolder and bolder. The prince whom I had taught to love the Church and to rule his lands with that love had decided to challenge the Pope. Louis decided that he, not the Pope, should be the person to appoint bishops to the churches that stood on his soil. The Pope was puzzled by Louis's behavior, but I was not. I did not have to look beyond his bedchamber to see where he had gotten the notion to set himself above the Pope. Eleanor's father had once tried appointing bishops to the churches in the Aquitaine. He had not succeeded; the Pope had removed the bishops and excommunicated Duke William. But William had been excommunicated several times for offenses against the Pope, and he never took it seriously. Eleanor, too, seemed to regard excommunication as an inconvenience, like wearing shoes that are too tight—uncomfortable but easily shucked off.

The Pope asked Abbot Bernard of Clairvaux to deal with the young king. Abbot Bernard was considered by some to be the holiest man of his day. (He got into

Heaven immediately after he died and became a Saint only nineteen years later, which is something of a record.)

Abbot Bernard wrote to Louis. Louis did not answer. Abbot Bernard came to see Louis to warn him that he was working for the Devil. Louis paid no attention. Abbot Bernard demanded that Louis remove his bishops. Louis refused. Abbot Bernard excommunicated Louis. Louis was not permitted to take holy communion; he was not allowed to pray. Louis was locked out of God's house.

Shortly after his excommunication, Louis's misdeeds reached a climax. That happened in a little town called Vitry.

Louis had acquired the cunning of a demon in planning his battles against the people of Champagne. He carefully surrounded the town of Vitry and set fire to the poor wooden houses with their thatched roofs. There was no quicker way to send the people outside their city walls and into surrender. But instead of fleeing outside, the people sought shelter inside their church.

Alas! The roof of the church, too, was wooden, and it caught some unhappy sparks from their homes. The roof collapsed, and everyone in the village died. Thirteen hundred people died like burnt offerings—on the altar of what? The altar of Louis's vanity? What was this sacrifice for? Louis took a new look at himself in the light of that fire. Was he meant to burn innocent people while his own soul stood close to the fires of Hell? Louis turned back from Vitry to home. To Paris. To me.

We met in my room. Louis trembled as he told me of his conflict with the Pope and what had happened at Vitry. The king was in a spiritual crisis. Now was not the time to punish him further. Now was the time to show him the kindness, the forgivingness of God. He should not be shoved back into the ways of the Church; he should want back in.

"Come, Louis," I said, "come see what I have built. Come see my beautiful new building."

"I am not allowed inside a church, Abbot. You forget that I have been excommunicated."

"You can come inside here, Louis; this church has not yet been consecrated. The space inside these walls does not yet belong to God."

As we walked around, I pointed out to him the many wonderful things I had invented, thanks be to God. I had discovered a way to raise the roof of a building so that the space inside shot Heavenward. I had found a way to place the supports for the ceiling outside the walls of my church; by freeing the walls from their duty of supporting a roof, I was able to make the walls of glass instead of heavy, dark stone. I used panels of colored glass that told stories from the Bible. When the sun came through the windows, I felt that I was standing inside of God's kaleidoscope.

"Abbot Bernard will not approve," Louis said.

"He might not, but he is curious enough to come to the consecration. Imagine! Why don't you come, too?"

"What makes you think, dear Suger, that Abbot Bernard would like to see two things he does not approve of, rather than just one."

I laughed. "It's true, neither you nor such an Earthly display of gold and jewels are favorites of the holy abbot. But come, my boy. Come. We may convince him otherwise."

"Shall I bring Eleanor?"

"By all means," I answered.

"Do you think Abbot Bernard will approve of her?"

"I cannot speak for Abbot Bernard, but I approve of her. Bring her. She is more decorative than any statue I have had carved, and I believe, dear Louis, that she is livelier than the play of light on any piece of stained glass. Besides, I can think of no one, man or woman, in all of Europe who so shares my love for fine things. I think such love brings us near to God."

"Abbott Bernard would say that such love comes between you and God."

I looked at the gold cross that the goldsmiths of

Lorraine had labored two years to finish. I rubbed it and thought that such sights on Earth were worth the cost of a few years in Heaven, but this was not the time to say anything like that to Louis, so I did not.

I wrote to Abbot Bernard and asked him to lift the ban of excommunication. I described Louis's humility and concern and promised that Louis would dismiss the bishops he had appointed. Louis dismissed the bishops, and the abbot lifted the ban.

In gratitude, Louis gave me the crystal and gold vase that Eleanor had given him as a wedding gift. I knew that Abbot Bernard would not approve of my keeping it, so I donated it to my church at St. Denis. (Certainly, God could not resent luxury that is dedicated to Him.) The crystal of the vase is cracked now, but people who visit the Louvre Museum still admire it. It stands there as an example of Eleanor's taste, of Louis's gratitude, and of my piety.

5

LOUIS AND ELEANOR arrived a day early for the consecration of my church. Louis wore a plain woolen robe and hood. Eleanor wore a gown of blue silk and a belt embroidered with gold and set with precious stones. The sleeves of her gown were long and fell back from her arms to expose her slender wrists, which she had sheathed in pale green silk. Louis could easily have been mistaken for a monk. Eleanor, however, could be taken for nothing but a queen. In bearing, in manner, in dress she was all queen.

Bishops had come from all over Europe. Rumors had long foretold that something new in the way of building would appear at St. Denis. Within a few years, the style that I, thanks be to God, developed at St. Denis became international. It showed up in churches all over Europe. Even today, colleges and churches are built in the style that I called modern, which people then called the style of Paris, but which men today call *Gothic*. Despicable word, *Gothic*. The Goths were pagans and had nothing to do with my church.

When the time came to carry the relics of our patron

saint, St. Denis, to their vault under the new altar, Louis helped to bear the load. His eagerness to be of service, his simple dress, his sincerity could not help but impress Abbot Bernard, and Abbot Bernard was not easily impressed with anything or anyone on Earth.

It had been said that Abbot Bernard could perform miracles, and Eleanor needed a miracle; she asked me to arrange an interview for her. It was not easy, for Abbot Bernard had little use for worldly queens, but my prestige was high at the moment, and so was King Louis's. Abbot Bernard consented to a short audience with her. I wondered if Eleanor would simplify her dress and her manner in order to impress him.

She did not.

They met in my quarters. Abbot Bernard, whose thoughts were always on high and whose eyes were always cast down, entered. Eleanor did not wait for the holy abbot to lift his eyes which was the signal that he was ready to talk. "Good day to you, Abbot," she said. Abbot Bernard's head jerked up. Eleanor waited for his eyes to catch hers. Then she smiled, a slow smile, a smile that spread as did her confidence.

"You wished to talk to me?" he asked.

"Yes, I did," she answered.

"About what?" he asked.

"I want you to give me a baby," she answered.

"Eleanor, please," I whispered, "surely you can find a

more delicate way to phrase that." Eleanor looked at me, surprised at my interruption, and then realized what she had said. She laughed out loud. No one ever laughed in the presence of Abbot Bernard. He had never been seen smiling, and he did not now. Eleanor realized that she must be more than serious, she must be solemn.

She repeated her request, quieter this time. "Abbot Bernard, I would that you could add your prayers to mine so that Louis and I should be granted a child."

Abbot Bernard lifted his head; his eyes, blue as Heaven, did not so much look at Eleanor as they penetrated her. "It is difficult for me to ask God to grant you children when your marriage is not valid in His eyes."

Eleanor was shocked. "What are you saying, Abbot Bernard?"

"I am saying only what you know: that you and King Louis are cousins within the fourth degree, and that degree is prohibited. You should never have married."

"But the Pope allowed it, he gave us special permission." Eleanor protested.

"Yes, he did," Abbot Bernard admitted, "but I did not recommend it."

Eleanor replied, "All my life I have been taught that the Pope is king of the Church. Bishops are his vassals, and I do believe that abbots are even lower than bishops.

What the Pope allows, certainly an abbot of Clairvaux should also allow. Louis and I have been married a week of years, and in your eyes we may not legally be married, but in the Pope's mind and in Louis's heart we are. I hold with that."

Men of great faith never argue. Abbot Bernard did not. He grabbed Eleanor's wrist and led her to a chair where he sat her down. Thus, with Queen Eleanor at an elevation lower than his, he spoke to her in a voice that was as loud as the Abbot's soul. He told her to work for peace within the kingdom, to learn to be an obedient wife, to quit meddling in the business of the Church, to curb her appetites for gold and jewels, for music and poetry, for color and luxury—for scarlet and miniver. He told her to do all this, and he would then add his voice to hers in prayer. Abbot Bernard's voice, it was known even then, went directly to Heaven, and rumor was that it never went unanswered.

Within a year after that interview, there was peace within the kingdom, and King Louis and Queen Eleanor had a child. The child was named Marie, in honor of the Lady to whom Eleanor had addressed her prayers. She had prayed only for a baby, whereas she should have asked for a baby *boy*. Oh, well, . . . next time.

The grand opening of St. Denis marked the welcome

of Louis back into the Church, the welcome of a baby girl into the royal household, the welcome of peace within the realm and, thanks be to God, the welcome of my beautiful, elegant, high new style of building churches.

6

EVEN THOUGH Louis had returned to the ways of the Church, he was still worried about his soul. He wanted to make up for his past—especially Vitry. When news reached us that Jerusalem stood in danger of falling into the hands of the Turks, Louis decided that he had found a way to make up for his bad behavior: he would gather together people from all over Europe to go on a great crusade to the Holy Land. They would save it from the Moslems.

It had been fifty years since the First Crusade. The men of that one had come from all over Europe and fought to establish a chain of kingdoms that stretched through Asia and Africa along the route to the Holy Land. These kingdoms insured Europeans safe passage into Jerusalem, for they were ruled by Frenchmen, younger brothers who welcomed a chance to rule something, somewhere. Eleanor's grandfather had been one of the men who had taken part in the First Crusade; his own second son, Raymond of Poitiers, was one of the men who had been given a kingdom overseas. This younger brother, this uncle of Eleanor's, was now ruler of Antioch.

He was only nine years older than Eleanor. They had played together when they were children. Raymond was very handsome; it was said that he could charm the curl out of a lady's hair—or into it—whichever he chose.

Eleanor and Louis came to tell me of their decision to go on Crusade. I did not approve.

"But, dear Suger," Louis said, "the Pope wants it. Abbot Bernard has preached for it; even Emperor Conrad of Germany has agreed to join. Eleanor is for it! She has been remarkable in signing up thousands of noblemen from the Aquitaine. She is anxious to go. Aren't you, my dear?" Louis looked at his wife and patted her hand as it rested on the arm of her chair.

I looked at Eleanor and smiled. She looked away, but she snapped her head back and looked me straight in the eye. It was not Eleanor's style to look away from the truth or the person asking it. "Let me talk to Eleanor alone," I said. Louis agreed and left the room.

"You have been bored, haven't you, my queen?" I asked.

"Yes, Abbot, I have," she answered. "Ever since Vitry, ever since Louis's return to the Church, I have been bored. There are no longer any troubadours allowed at the castle. There is no music. Louis has taken down the tapestries from our room. He himself dresses like a monk. My life is silent and without color."

"What about your daughter, Marie?"

"Oh, she is a joy! But, Abbot, I am a grown woman. I have need for sounds not found in a baby's gurgle and for sights outside the nursery walls. Show me a woman who is content to be in the company of babies all day, and I'll show you a woman who is . . . who is . . ."

"Is what, Eleanor?"

"Is an Adelaide—my mother-in-law."

"What about the life of the intellect, Eleanor? What about learning? Paris is the place for that."

"And so is the Aquitaine, Abbot. And so is Jerusalem and so is Constantinople." Eleanor rose from her chair and walked across the room away from me. She turned, her arms folded across her chest. "Just as there are men of action," she continued, "there are women of action, too. I am one of those! I need to move, to travel. I like to read the character of a man from the lines of his face not from the lines of a book. I like to feel foreign air on my face. I want to go on Crusade. Boredom is a deadly sin, Abbot, and I am bored. Does not my soul matter, too?"

"Eleanor, Eleanor! Calm down. Let me tell you of my objections. A Crusade is a fancy name for war. War means killing. Not only men are killed, but their ideas die, too. And the art that could be born of those ideas never sees day."

"But a Crusade, dear Abbot, will give all of France a thorough flushing. How else can you rid Europe of its criminals, its beggars, its restless younger sons, and not only ship them out but also rescue their souls. Anyone who dies on Crusade is guaranteed admission into Heaven. Besides, we'll save Jerusalem. By any measure, a Crusade is a bargain."

I laughed. "How can I hold out against a saintly abbot, a king and a pope? And a beautiful, restless queen besides?"

"Don't try. We need you on our side, Abbot Suger. Louis is appointing you head of the government of France for the time that we will be gone."

"I feel honored, your majesty."

"Feel honored now, dear Abbot, for you will soon feel overworked."

"You will see much and learn much, Eleanor. Don't let the glitter of the East blind you to plain goodness."

"I can not only see plainness, I can smell it, and I don't like it. And as for goodness, I like it salted with greatness. Louis is *good*, Abbot; he is very *good*. The Orient is famous for its spices, Abbot. Do you think that good Louis can find some flavor over there?"

"Eleanor, don't mistake simplicity for simple-mindedness."

"Oh, Abbot, how could I? True simplicity is elegant. Can you imagine me not loving anything that is truly elegant?"

I laughed. She was a match for anyone, that queen. Anyone, except a confused man. I called Louis back into the room.

"Louis, my king, my son, go with my blessing. Odo the Chaplain will accompany you. He will be your confessor as well as my messenger. I shall send you my blessings through him. Now, while I have you within my sight, let me bless you both and your mission."

They knelt, and I placed my hands over their heads, thinking of what different materials those heads were made: Louis's, filled with dreams of a holy life; Eleanor's, with dreams for which Louis did not even have names.

7

THE DIFFERENCES between Louis and Eleanor were apparent from the very start of the Crusade. Louis rode at the rear of the long caravan. Eleanor rode up front. Louis considered simplicity of dress a duty. Eleanor carried every comfort that was portable: candles, cosmetics, clothing. The luggage of Eleanor and her lady friends took as many wagons as the arms of the men who were to do battle for Jerusalem. The ladies soon earned a nickname; they were called *The Amazons*.

Odo wrote me faithfully. From his letters I kept track of their progress. Eleanor rode through every foreign town, able to spot some sight to store in her memory. There was no new place that she could not enjoy for its differences. At last they reached Constantinople. There have been glorious cities and beautiful ones before and since Constantinople, but nothing in all of history has ever matched its magnificence. Ancient Athens was beautiful but austere. Rome was great but governmental. Constantinople was gay, and it glittered. It was as if the whole city had been lifted in a piece and then dipped into a rainbow. But not a pastel rainbow, a rainbow of undiluted color.

It was not only a city of color but also of ceremonies. Each meal, each greeting, was like a small brilliant tile that was part of an elaborate mosaic. And mosaics! They were all over Constantinople, on walls and ceilings and floors. The floors of the palaces were covered with thick carpets; the best floors of Europe wore only rushes. Constantinople straddled both Europe and Asia, and its shops supplied the best of both civilizations. The streets were paved, and the houses had baths. Everyone who lived in Constantinople considered the Crusaders as a new generation of barbaric invaders, they seemed that primitive.

Eleanor usually enjoyed contrasts, but she did not enjoy seeing plain Louis look like a country boy beside the smooth, handsome, elaborately dressed Manuel Comnenus, the ruler of Constantinople. Louis helped his men saddle horses and helped load the baggage carts; he could never do enough to prove that he was serving both God and man. Louis was uncomfortable with all ceremonies except those of the Church. Manuel Comnenus had servants who served his servants. Manuel Comnenus sat upon a throne of gold; and his vassals did not kneel at his feet, they lay down at his feet. Manuel Comnenus expected it, and no one ever questioned it. Compared to Constantinople, court life in Paris seemed like life in Noah's ark.

There was no meal in Constantinople in which Eleanor did not taste something new and different and delicious. And the same could be said of her days; they were full of strange spices that she, more than any woman of her time, was ready to try, to memorize, to adopt, to adapt. Ten days they stayed in Constantinople. Only ten days. Ten days that Eleanor held onto and that Louis pulled away from, ten days that unraveled the ties between the king and queen of France.

"Louis, my husband," Eleanor said, "have you noticed the throne upon which Manuel sits?"

"Indeed I have."

"It is made of gold, pure gold, and it is encrusted with precious stones."

"That," Louis said, "is not what I noticed. I do not see the gold of which his throne is built. I see the deceit. He reeks of the sweet perfume of deceit. I fear that he has made an alliance with the Turks. We must leave Constantinople and join Emperor Conrad's forces."

"Can we stay just a few days more? I would like to purchase some of the carpets they use here. I think that carpets would do a lot for French floors and French feet."

"No, Eleanor; we leave tomorrow. Without carpets."

Constantinople was the rich & beautiful fortress of Christianity in the East

"Only a few days more, Louis. Manuel just brought you news that Emperor Conrad and his Germans have just had a great victory over the Turks."

"I am not sure of that. I do not believe that truth is a habit with Manuel."

Eleanor laughed. "You are right, dear Louis. I notice that his lips speak to his dowdy wife, Bertha—really, she ought to learn to do something with makeup—while his eyes smile at his niece, Theodora. But, Louis, if you are sure a man is lying, you know all you need to know of him. To know another man's weakness gives you strength. Deal with him on his terms, or let me do it. The Aquitaine breeds this kind of man as readily as cow dung breeds flies! Let us stay. Let me do each thing just one more time. One more time falconing in Manuel's forest. One more time feasting. . . ."

"We're leaving tomorrow. We could leave this afternoon, and we would, if you women knew how to travel light."

Eleanor laughed. "Louis, my dear, I refuse to arrive in Antioch to greet my Uncle Raymond looking like Manuel's frumpy Bertha. And I can tell you, my husband king, that if it had taken five sumpter trains to carry my wardrobe into Constantinople, it would have been worth it. I am as uncomfortable plain as you are fancy. I don't know whether you bring up the rear of the caravan because you are dressed for the part or whether you are dressed for the part because you bring up the rear."

"I will hear no more, Eleanor. We leave in the morning."

"Do you think Manuel will mind if I take a few of his carpets as souvenirs? We can roll them up and tuck them here and there in my sumpter trains."

"Eleanor! Thou shalt not steal."

"But whatever harm I do my soul by stealing, I shall make up for by the help and comfort I shall do my feet. Feet have soles, too."

"You will hardly enter Heaven on feet that have walked on stolen carpets."

"And you will hardly learn to take a joke."

With that, Eleanor turned her back to Louis and left the room.

8

GREAT WAS THE DISTANCE that separated the beginning of the caravan from its end, but greater still was the distance that separated the attitude of the forward queen from the attitude of the backward king. Both distances were to cause trouble outside of Constantinople.

The Crusaders had not traveled far before they met some remnants of Emperor Conrad's army. Manuel had indeed lied. There had been no victory at all for the German army; they had been led into an ambush by the guides that Manuel had recommended. Their supplies of food and water had been too short for a desert trip; the Turks knew it, and they swept down on the thirsty army. The Turks were swift and vicious. When Louis met the scattered, tattered remnants of the German army, they were returning to Constantinople, ready to go home. Only by bribery and promises did Louis convince Conrad not to give up the Crusade altogether.

Louis wrote to me asking for more money. He had done so several times before. Each loaf of bread that the Crusaders had to buy was purchased at an inflated price, and now in addition, Louis had to pay off the Germans to keep them from abandoning the Crusade.

It was an ordeal to travel through the mountains that covered their route. Their caravan was long, longer than most, because of the amount of luggage required by Eleanor and her Amazons. It was difficult for the rear of the caravan to know what the front was doing. The mountain peaks made it difficult to travel in a straight line. The women often had to be carried because they could not handle their horses on the steep slopes.

Eleanor rode up front as usual. There was little about this part of the trip that appealed to her, especially after the magic of Constantinople. It was not her way to sulk, however. A bad mood was nothing but a curtain between her and life, and she did not want to waste even an uncomfortable trip through the mountains. She would enjoy the trip as best she could, she decided. And the scenery. She would enjoy that, too.

In the morning Louis gave orders to the lead wagons telling them the stopping place for the night. He urged all the troops to stay in close file; after all, they were strangers in a strange land. On the day of Epiphany, January 6, Louis told the forward vans to stop at a high flatland, which scouts had spotted over the next peak.

Eleanor emerged from her van to stretch her legs. As she walked around the table of land that she was to call home for the night, she looked over its far edge and saw below her a valley that looked like a sudden springtime.

"Oh, Geoffrey," she called to the leader of the forward van, "come look!"

Geoffrey of Rancon, who was one of Eleanor's loyal lords from Aquitaine, interrupted what he was doing and came to his queen's side. "Look below," Eleanor commanded. "Doesn't that pert little valley seem more like home than this pale, dry plain?"

"Yes, my queen, it does," Geoffrey of Rancon answered.

"I think it would be far nicer to spend the night there."

"But, your majesty, the king gave orders for us to make camp here."

"Did the king see this valley?"

"No, your majesty. He had only the word of his scouts; they recommended the plateau."

"Yes, the king's scouts seemed convinced that there is no place for comfort in Christianity. Come, we will descend into the valley to make camp."

"But, Queen Eleanor, the king gave orders . . ."

Eleanor looked around her. "Come, Geoffrey of Rancon, we will camp on God's green earth tonight. I swear that Heaven sucked all the juice of life from this plain because he didn't want man on it," she muttered.

"Your majesty," Geoffrey of Rancon began again.

"Yes? What now?"

"The king has given orders for us to stay in close ranks. It is difficult to reckon direction among these mountain peaks. It is absolutely necessary that we stay close together."

"Who said that we shall not?" Eleanor asked. "The king will come up to the plain and not find us, then he will look below as I just have and see us, and then he will follow. And we shall all sleep close and cozy tonight. Give the order to move on."

Eleanor's decision took no longer than it takes me to tell of it, and for that reason, no one in that advance train had time to spot the Turks who were lurking in the mountains that surrounded the plain.

Awkward would be the softest possible description of the path the men in the rearward party had had to follow to reach the flat plateau. Knights had shed their armor to ease their ascent. King Louis brought up the rear of the vans, working, sweating, heaving, and at last, looking for Eleanor; she was nowhere to be found on the whole of the plateau. Louis feared the worst. As he and his men swarmed around looking for the lost forward van, the Turks found their chance. They galloped down from the mountains where they had been watching and waiting.

It was a slaughter. Louis's men were caught unarmed, unarmored and exhausted from their climb.

Louis fought bravely. Without the glamour and the trappings of a king, he fought like one. Eleanor did not know it. Neither did the Turks know that they were fighting the King of the Franks. That the Turks did not know was fortunate; had they known that the plainly clad brave leader was King of the Franks, they would have taken him prisoner, and they would then have held him for ransom. A king's ransom.

Meanwhile, night fell at Eleanor's camp, and Louis and his men did not appear. One man, then two, then a few more straggled in, and the tales they told prepared Eleanor for the worst. She realized that she might at that very moment be a widow.

At daybreak Odo the Chaplain led the king into the queen's camp. Louis was riding a pack animal. The weary king walked into his wife's tent. Eleanor smiled, relieved. Her husband had survived.

Louis saw the smile but not its reason. He was exhausted and heartbroken. "Well, Eleanor," he said, "can you tell me why I find you on this side of the mountain instead of up above?"

"My dear husband, you know that the grass always looks greener on the other side of the mountain, and you see, it is indeed greener here in this valley."

Louis had had enough of his wife's wit. He lost patience. As he lost patience, he seemed to lose weariness, too. He swung around and ordered Odo to find the leader of the forward van, Geoffrey of Rancon.

When Geoffrey appeared, the king shouted, "You, sir, are guilty of treason. You have disobeyed orders, and you shall hang in the morning."

Eleanor, above all things, was honest. "Louis, I am afraid that if you hang my vassal, Geoffrey of Rancon, you must also hang his duchess. For I am more to blame than is he."

"Hang you?"

"Yes, Geoffrey acted under orders, my orders; it was I, not he, who disobeyed. Geoffrey of Rancon was merely following the commands of his duchess, his queen . . ." Eleanor paused a minute and added, "and yours."

Louis paused. His arms fell to his side. "All right, Eleanor. Geoffrey of Rancon shall not hang. He shall leave the Crusade and return home in disgrace."

"And am I to return home, too, my king?"

"No, Eleanor," Louis said, "I have a worse punishment in store for you. You will continue on the Crusade."

"But that is hardly punishment. I love travel."

"But you shall also show some restraint. And I know you do not like that. You and your lady friends, your Amazons, will control your whims and become obedient pilgrims. Plain pilgrims, I may add."

"Aye, my lord," Eleanor said.

"Tomorrow we will climb down from these treacherous mountains and go to Antioch by sea."

"Why not?" Eleanor said. "We've traveled over mountains, along the seashore, and across a plateau. Now it's down to the sea. I am grateful, my lord, that you cannot stretch your wings and fly; the air is the only route to the Holy Land we have not tried."

Louis said, "Your bad behavior will end with that remark. Tomorrow we close ranks and head for port, and you, Eleanor, will close your mouth and do likewise."

Eleanor was struck dumb. Louis had never spoken to her like that. But she smiled. Perhaps, she had married a king after all.

9

ELEANOR'S NEW HUMILITY did not last. The Crusaders had to stay in a dirty port town on the coast while they rented enough boats to make the journey to Antioch. Eleanor's impatience warmed, percolated and boiled over during the three weeks' wait. She did not like stink or squalor, and the port town had too much of both.

At last they sailed for Antioch. When they reached port, Raymond was there to greet them. Eleanor had not seen her uncle in a decade. He was handsome and daring and gay, and he shared Eleanor's exquisite taste in dress and furnishings and art. It took only the ten-mile trip from the harbor to the castle for Eleanor and her uncle to make up for the ten years they had not seen each other. Eleanor emerged from that ride as saucy as the Amazon who had started out on Crusade.

Antioch appealed to Eleanor. Why would it not? It had as much history as Constantinople, almost as much commerce, and it was even more beautiful. It was more like home. Like the Aquitaine. The stiffness of court life, which Eleanor had seen and had practiced in Constantinople, was softened by her relaxed, high-spirited uncle. What a man was Raymond.

What a man! He showered his guests with gifts. Wines cooled with mountain snow, perfumes, cloths and jewels. He had the openhandedness that comes in men who love to share their great good taste with others.

Raymond also had other reasons for being generous. His other reasons were political. He wanted Louis's forces to join his to recover Edessa. After all, he argued, no road to Jerusalem was safe for Christians as long as Edessa was held by Moslems. Louis realized that although Jerusalem was in danger of falling as long as the Turks held Edessa, Antioch, which was even closer, was threatened far more. Louis could see that even though he would be helping Jerusalem a great deal by helping Edessa, he would be helping Raymond more. He was not anxious to do that. He resented Raymond; he resented the cozy, shared laughter of his wife and her uncle. Louis was jealous.

The noblemen who were Louis's vassals resented Eleanor, too. They held her and her willful ways and her Amazons responsible for the tragedy that had overcome them that dreadful day on the plateau. They held her even more responsible than that. Had it not been for her, Louis would never have gone to war years before; and had he never gone to war, he never would have done what he did at Vitry; and had he never done what he did at Vitry, he would never have felt the need to go on Crusade; and if he had never needed to go on Crusade, neither would they; and if they had not gone on Crusade, they would not be halfway across the world now trying to help her fancy Uncle Raymond. Even though Raymond's plan made military sense, they urged Louis to take Damascus instead. Was it not Louis's soul, not Raymond's precious Antioch, that was to be saved?

Louis turned Raymond down, and Raymond flew into a rage—a rage for which only Eleanor had any sympathy. She told Odo that she and her uncle wanted a private audience with Louis; he was to stand guard at the door and keep all others out.

Raymond began the conference by reviewing the wisdom of his plan to recapture Edessa. Louis listened. Raymond's plan was well laid out. It was sound. It made sense, but Louis turned it down again. "My advisers and I have decided to take Damascus."

"I urge you to reconsider," Raymond said.

"We will go to Damascus," Louis repeated.

"But, Louis . . ." Raymond began.

Eleanor interrupted, "My husband suffers from a complaint common to weak men: he will not change his mind once his advisers have made it up for him."

Louis got up from his chair. "We will leave for Damascus in the morning."

"I shall not," Eleanor said.

"I said *we* will leave in the morning," Louis repeated.

"I am staying in Antioch," Eleanor said.

Raymond smiled.

Louis saw the smile and his pride, as a husband and as a king, could not allow him to be smiled at in the manner of Raymond or be spoken to in the manner of Eleanor.

"You will leave with me in the morning, Eleanor. You are my vassal and my wife, and that makes two sets of laws that grant me sovereignty over you."

Eleanor replied, "I am your vassal, sir, only because you hold my lands. And you hold my lands only because I am your wife. But watch that, Louis, watch that! Because there are those who say that in the eyes of Heaven I am not your wife."

"Who says that?" Raymond asked.

"Abbot Bernard for one. Abbot Bernard says that my husband and I are cousins within the fourth degree, and therefore we are living in sin. Abbot Bernard says that in the eyes of God, Louis and I are not husband and wife."

"But the Pope . . ." Louis stammered.

"The Pope looked the other way when we married, Louis. And so did you. Your passions and my possessions overcame your conscience. Take another look at our family trees, I say, and then tell me whether I am your wife."

Louis was badly shaken. Raymond's smile broadened. Louis looked from him to Eleanor and then said, in a low, steady voice, "Pack your things, Duchess of Aquitaine. We leave Antioch in the morning, and we leave together."

Louis then called to Odo. "Please see that the queen has an escort to her room this evening, kind Odo. She will need a good rest for her journey tomorrow. Please see to it that there is a guard at her door so that no one may enter or leave her room. If she complains of being too tired to emerge in the morning, see to it that she is carried to Damascus."

10

THE PLAN to take Damascus was a failure. The pilgrims had to make their way to Jerusalem without victory. Louis refused to wear his crown in the city where our Lord had worn the Crown of Thorns. (An elegant gesture, I thought.) Odo's letters were full of Louis's worries: about Eleanor, about his marriage, about the fate of Jerusalem.

I could do nothing about saving Jerusalem, but I did what I could to save the marriage. I wrote to the Pope and told him of the serious quarrel that had occurred between Eleanor and Louis. Then I wrote to Louis and urged him to return home by way of Rome. I suggested that a visit to the Pope would give Eleanor and him a chance to renew their marriage vows. A chance to begin again.

My plan worked. The Pope had long talks with them both and reassured Louis that the Church was always willing to grant special permission when a marriage served so much good. He told them that he wanted to hear no more talk of cousins, that the word was not to be mentioned in their conversations again. Louis was relieved. He and Eleanor made up. They then asked the Pope to urge God to grant them an heir.

Eleanor and Louis returned to Paris in November, and they had another child, but not a future king. Another girl, whom they named Alix.

While they had been gone, I had, thanks be to God, beautifully redecorated the royal palace, but the winter of their return was a cold one. Cold for Paris, but colder still compared to Constantinople and Antioch. Eleanor came to see me; she lacked her usual smile, her usual high color.

"What is the matter?" I asked. "You look pale, my lady."

"Why should I not, Abbott? My husband has drained the color from everything else. His world is all black and white, right and wrong."

"He has grown, Eleanor. He is much more a king than the man you married fifteen years ago."

"Ha! Abbot. I thought I married a king, and I find I married a monk."

"What else is bothering you, Eleanor?"

"The gray color of life at our court. The tastelessness of everything. Louis now eats the plain fare of the monks; he dines with them instead of with me. Abbot, I, too, have grown. I am much more a queen now than I was in those days when I was sending Louis into the Aquitaine and into Champagne to do battle for my every whim. I have learned a great deal. I want to use what I have learned. I want to be a queen, one who sets a pattern for life in the land. One who gives tone and tune to her country. And now that I have learned so much, Louis will not listen to me." She looked down at her lap and said, "Besides, I don't love Louis."

"But what has marriage to do with love, Eleanor? Marriage is a land contract not a love match."

"I keep thinking it can be something more. I have much more than land to give."

"For my sake, Eleanor, stay with Louis. Come here, come to me, to my church, when you need to see beautiful things, when you need to talk about the glories of Constantinople. I can be your confessor for all things."

"Yes, for all things. Dear Suger, dear, dear Suger. Abbot Bernard says that to love beautiful carvings is to worship idols, but you tell me that love of such beauty leads to love of God. To Abbot Bernard, I am living in sin with my cousin-husband. To you, I am holding the realm together."

"Visit me often, Eleanor."

"Yes, Abbot. You shall be my specialist."

"In all things, Eleanor. Thanks be to God, I am a specialist in everything."

"Abbot Suger, you shall spend time in Hell for your lack of modesty." Eleanor laughed. Her laughter had some of its former naughtiness, and I couldn't help but join in.

Back in Heaven

ELEANOR was sitting on a cloud, hugging her knees. Abbot Suger smiled down at her. "You know I loved those long visits of yours. They were the joy of my last months on Earth. What happened after I died, Eleanor? Why did you not stay with Louis?"

"Oh, I don't know," Eleanor said. She rested her forehead on her knees and then turned her head toward Abbot Suger. "Your not being there made a difference," she said, smiling.

"That's not what made the big difference," boomed Matilda-Empress.

Abbot Suger turned to look at Matilda-Empress and then said, "Are you going to tell me what made the big difference?"

"Eleanor met my son Henry, and she fell madly in love with him. It's as simple as that."

"Not quite that simple, Mother Matilda. Nothing in our century was that simple. There was my boredom with life at Louis's court. And there was always the Aquitaine."

"Move over," Matilda-Empress said. The tiny abbot

moved to the left, Eleanor moved to the right; the cloud compressed as Matilda-Empress sat between them. She glared at her daughter-in-law. "I'll tell it as I saw it," she said.

"There is no other way to tell a story," the abbot answered as he settled himself deeper into the cloud.

Part two
Matilda-Empress's Tale

1

IN THE SUMMER following the death of Abbot Suger, my husband, Geoffrey, went to the French court to pay homage to Louis. He took our son Henry with him. Geoffrey, my husband, was Count of Anjou; everyone called him Geoffrey Plantagenet because he always wore a stalk of that beautiful wild broom, *planta genista*, in his hat. Henry, our son, had picked up the habit, so he was called Plantagenet, too. It became our family name.

Geoffrey, my husband, was also called Geoffrey the Fair because he was handsome; he knew it. Henry, my son, was also handsome; he knew it, too.

There were a lot of things that Geoffrey could have done but did not. He could have joined Louis on Crusade, but he did not. He could have paid homage to Louis years before, but he did not. Geoffrey never did anything that did not suit his purposes, his immediate purposes.

Neither love nor loyalty brought Geoffrey to court at that late date to pay homage to his king and queen. Necessity brought him. Henry, our son, had been named Duke of Normandy. In order for him to collect the taxes on his lands, he needed the royal stamp of approval; Henry needed to pay homage to his overlord, King Louis, and at the same time receive the kiss of peace from his king.

Henry's good looks may have come from his father, but his important titles came from me—Matilda, daughter of King Henry I of England and granddaughter of the man who even today was the last successful conqueror of England. Before he had invaded England in the year 1066, my grandfather was called William the Bastard because he was. After the year 1066, he was called William the Conqueror because he was.

When Stephen, the present king of England died, the crown would go to Henry, my son. Stephen was my worthless nephew. I had kept alive my claim to the throne by making a lot of noise about it both in England and France, and by lining up barons and lords who pledged their support to me. Geoffrey and I thought it would be a good idea to get Henry engaged to Marie, the daughter of Eleanor and Louis. Marie was five years old at the time. Abbot Bernard of Clairvaux, however, said that he could never allow a marriage between our son, Henry, and any daughter of Eleanor. "Cousins," he said. It seems that the Abbot Bernard found *cousins* in any marriage of which he did not approve. I was tempted to ask him whom he thought Cain and Abel had married, but Geoffrey made me hold my tongue. He was already in enough trouble with the abbot. Abbot Bernard had recently had him excommunicated.

The Abbot Bernard made a habit of doing that to my husband. It was always done more for politics than religion. Bernard always sided with Louis in any quarrels that came up between Louis and Geoffrey. And now that Louis had returned from the Crusade and now that Abbot Suger was dead, Abbot Bernard was always using the Church as a club over Geoffrey's head. What had Geoffrey done that was so terrible? I put his case before you:

For three years King Louis's steward had been attacking our castles in the Vexin. The Vexin was a little wedge of land between our Normandy and Louis's France. The Vexin was not large, but it was important. Geoffrey was unable to do anything in return because of the Truce of God. The Truce of God was an order from the Pope, which said that no one was allowed to attack the lands of any lords who were on Crusade.

As soon as Louis returned from Crusade, Geoffrey went right to the source of the trouble. He poured boiling oil on the rafters of the steward's very own castle; then he fired flaming arrows at it. People poured out of the castle along with the flames. One who came running was the steward himself. Geoffrey caught him like a runaway puppy and put him in a dungeon. Abbot Bernard was shocked. No one, he said, could treat an officer of the king that way. Geoffrey said that he could. Bernard ordered Geoffrey to release the steward. Geoffrey said no. So Abbot Bernard excommunicated Geoffrey. Geoffrey was determined to prove his point. He brought the steward to the castle in chains. Abbot Bernard, who was at court with Eleanor and Louis, was amazed at his nerve. He called him brazen.

There they were: Queen Eleanor, King Louis and Abbot Bernard on one side. Geoffrey, Henry and the steward (in chains) on the other.

Geoffrey bowed. "I came, your majesty, to pay homage to you and your lady and to request that you recognize my son, Henry, as Duke of Normandy." He said all this very solemnly even as he was holding the rope that bound the hands of his prisoner—like a palfrey on a leash.

Abbot Bernard answered, "Give up your prisoner, Count Geoffrey, and I shall lift the ban of excommunication from you, and King Louis will recognize your son as Duke of Normandy."

"Give up my prisoner? What has holding a prisoner that is rightfully mine to do with my son's collecting the taxes that are rightfully his?"

One look from the fierce blue eyes of Bernard was usually enough for most people. Most people believed that the blue of his eyes was the fire of Heaven. "Give up your prisoner," Abbot Bernard repeated. "It is a sin to keep your king's steward in chains."

Geoffrey answered, "I refuse to free him. I got him legally."

"It is a sin to keep him," Abbot Bernard repeated.

"If it is a sin to keep him, I refuse to be excused from that sin." And with that Geoffrey turned his back on king, queen and abbot and stomped out of the room, pulling the steward behind him.

Eleanor who had been sitting listlessly at the beginning of the interview came to attention. Geoffrey was a man she could understand. Geoffrey was a man like her father; he knew how to talk to an abbot. Talk *back* to an abbot.

"Beware, Count of Anjou," Bernard called after Geoffrey. "Beware what shall befall you."

Eleanor now looked more closely at Henry. Like father like son? She remembered hearing that when Abbot Bernard had looked at Henry when he was only an infant, the Abbot had said, "From the Devil he came and to the Devil he will go." If Abbot Bernard had that to say about Henry, Eleanor could not but believe that here was a man she could love.

Henry bowed out of the room, and shortly thereafter Eleanor asked to be excused.

Geoffrey and Henry were riding out of Paris when Eleanor's messenger caught up with them; Eleanor wanted a meeting, alone. They met, Geoffrey, Henry and Eleanor; they met in a field outside of town, a place to which Eleanor could ride. Eleanor never looked better than when she was riding. The fresh air brought color to her face. Her color, her vitality, were no match for her years. Eleanor was now thirty. Henry was eighteen. But an older woman can bring important experience to a marriage contract. A lady's age is never a measure of her youth. It did not matter, for example, that I was fifteen years older than my husband, Geoffrey the Fair.

Eleanor was a woman who had seen the world and had profited by it. Henry was a man who could value her experience. I had taught him that. I had taught my son to surround himself with people of learning and experience. Louis was too thickheaded to use this valuable tool, this queen, this restless beauty, this Eleanor.

They talked, the three of them. And they came to an agreement.

When Geoffrey reappeared at court a week later and released the king's steward, both the king and the abbot considered themselves very persuasive. After a few more days, they completed peace talks, and Geoffrey gave up the Vexin. The king and the abbot congratulated themselves again. Then Bernard lifted the ban of excommunication from Geoffrey, and the king accepted homage from Henry.

Eleanor watched the homage ceremony. Henry knelt before his king, placed his hands in Louis's palms, and swore to protect the king from his enemies. As Henry's face peered over first one shoulder and then the other, receiving from Louis the kiss of peace, Henry smiled up at Eleanor. Eleanor winked. Geoffrey noticed. Abbot Bernard did not; King Louis did not; self-righteous people never looked beyond themselves for the reasons that things happen.

2

A FEVER KILLED my husband as he and Henry were returning from court. Abbot Bernard said that it was Divine Justice, but I don't think it was. If Geoffrey were the sinner that Abbot Bernard believed him to be, why would he die *after* he had been restored to the Church? I did not believe Abbot Bernard. It was a fever, an accident, a trick of Fate, that killed my husband Geoffrey after he had made peace at the court of the Capets.

3

ON THE FIRST DAY of spring in the year 1152 Eleanor and Louis were separated. Eleanor felt that she was casting off two winters. Louis declared that he still loved her, but Abbot Bernard told the king that it was time for him to put aside his love for Eleanor; she had long ago put aside her love for him. Abbot Bernard reminded Louis that the best part of his marriage to Eleanor would stay with him; their daughters, Marie and Alix, were to remain in Paris. Abbot Bernard also reminded Louis that he had another love, his love of the Church, to substitute for his love of Eleanor; Eleanor, he said, had no love to substitute for him.

Abbot Bernard did not know about Henry.

He soon found out.

Eleanor and Henry were married less than two months after Eleanor had received her separation.

Bernard was shocked. The king was shamed. Abbot Bernard recommended excommunication. Louis's advisers recommended war. After all, Eleanor was still Louis's vassal, and as such, she had no right to marry without his consent. Louis listened to his advisers. He attempted an invasion of Normandy, his ex-wife's new home.

Henry swept them back like fuzz before a broom.

"Ah," Eleanor laughed when she heard the outcome of the battle, "a broom of Plantagenet sweeps clean."

Eleanor knew that at last she had a mate whose energy and decisiveness matched hers.

4

AND HENRY did not hesitate to use Eleanor as she wished to be used. He put her in charge of the lands that he could not directly supervise. He had some quarrels with his cousin Stephen, that worthless nephew of mine, who had stolen the throne from me. While he was in England settling feuds, Eleanor collected taxes and administered castles and dispensed justice in the courts of Normandy and Anjou as well as in her own Aquitaine.

As Eleanor did all this, she also refurnished her castles with linens and embroideries and gold plate; she also provided a home for all the troubadours that Louis had banished from his realm. The courts of Eleanor as Duchess of Normandy and Aquitaine were beautiful and efficient. She wasted nothing that she learned. And to an ambitious, restless man like my son, she was an asset, the asset that Eleanor had always known she could be, given half a chance.

She and Henry often went falconing together, they often held court together; they were suited to each other and to their times as no other couple in history.

And they had a son. Eleanor regarded the birth of that first son as final evidence that she and Henry were right for each other and for Normandy, Anjou, and the Aquitaine, and when the time would come, they would be right for England.

On December 7, 1154
Henry and Eleanor
crossed the stormy
Channel to claim their
crowns to the English throne.

5

THEN STEPHEN, my worthless nephew, who had taken the throne of England from me, died. Stephen had made his lords and barons agree to accept Henry as king. Of course, Stephen only did that because of constant pressure from me and only after his own greedy son, Eustace, had managed to choke to death on a plate of eels.

Stephen had almost wrecked that fair island. And he would have if he had lived much longer, and if the English people were not of the common sense good stock that they are.

"Just think!" Henry said. "We are married only a little more than two years, and I have made you a queen."

"Louis and I were married less than two weeks when he made me one," Eleanor replied.

"My family has a habit of holding onto its gains."

"Really, sir?" Eleanor said stepping up close to Henry.

"Yes," Henry answered. Then he grabbed Eleanor and hugged her so that she thought she would not emerge from his arms without several broken bones.

But she did.

Henry assembled men and ships and made ready to set sail across the English Channel to claim his crown. But the winter weather made passage difficult. Henry looked out at the English Channel as if it were a moat, meant to keep him out of his own castle.

Day after day passed in that small harbor town as the men and ships waited. At every minute of every day, someone would be looking to see if the skies would clear, but they did not. The storms continued.

At last Henry gave orders for everyone to man the boats. Fair weather or foul, he would cross the Channel; he had waited long enough. Henry thrust his fist into the air as if to punch the sky back and said, "Dear God, let us ride this storm together. England needs us."

Eleanor smiled. Henry's prayers were like her father's; both regarded God as a companion, and neither ever questioned His being on his side.

The crossing was wretched, but Eleanor did not complain. She held their young son in her arms for the time it took to cross. When at last their tiny fleet came ashore on the English isle, the ships were scattered among the ports of the coast like billiard balls into various pockets.

That their new king came to them through wind and

storm did much to endear him to the people. They welcomed King Henry II and his Queen Eleanor.

The coronation ceremony took place in Westminster Abbey in December. That great old church was another part of England that Stephen had allowed to go to ruin, so the ceremony, beautiful as it was, was like conducting a symphony in an abandoned stable.

6

ELEANOR AND I had no great love for each other. Two women cannot love the same man and also love each other. But Eleanor and I had respect for each other. Where love is not possible, respect will do. I admired Eleanor's efficiency and her willingness to learn. No longer was she the ambitious, spoiled young Queen of the Franks. Now she was energetic, and her energies were well directed.

Discomfort, bad weather, even pregnancy did not stop her. Eleanor bore eight children within the fifteen years I knew her. And of those, only the first, little William, died while I still lived. Even as she embarked on that rough Channel crossing, she was pregnant with their second child and second son; they named him Henry. Their next child they named for me: Matilda. Then followed Richard, whom everyone knows as Richard the Lion Heart. Geoffrey came a year later, followed by Eleanor, Joanna and finally John. John was the last of their children and the last of an era.

An era. It was almost that. Eleanor and Henry squeezed a great deal of living into a single week, even into a single day. Since taxes were as often paid in merchandise as they were in money, Eleanor and Henry and the whole royal household often moved from one castle to another to use up their share of a manor's profits. Barley, potatoes and cattle could not be mailed.

And take the question of loyalty. Henry believed that people need to see who they are working for, fighting for. He must not merely be a name. He must be a face. (Doesn't every corporation display pictures of its president, and doesn't every government office in the United States have a picture of the President?) In those days there were no pictures, so the king and queen came in person. They held court, and at these courts they collected homage and taxes, but they also allowed people to tell their grievances.

Eleanor knew people. She was a psychologist before there was even a word for it. She knew that if a man paid homage to someone who was magnificent, he thought better of himself than if he paid homage to someone who was simple. What she had begun to learn about impressing people in the Aquitaine, she had finished learning in Constantinople. But there was no pretense in her manners, for luxury was a necessity to Eleanor.

She imported incense and burned it to do battle with the terrible odors that hugged the ground in London's fog. She served wine at her table instead of beer. She furnished her castles with pillows stuffed with down and covered with silk, and she employed her beloved musicians and poets. She found the English a cheerful race, but plain. Good businessmen, but plain. Good storytellers, but plain. Eleanor followed her own sound aristocratic tastes, and the nation gratefully followed. Nothing in England has been the same since.

But it was the matter of justice that kept the king and queen most busy, kept them most on the road, and often kept them in separate parts of the kingdom. Everyone was at war with everyone else. Robbers haunted the forests of Sherwood, and the legend of Robin Hood began. The law on one side of a road was different from the law on the other. The island was in chaos. It was my son's job to pull it all together and to be clever about it. Henry did, and Henry was.

There was an old law in England that allowed people to appeal to the king if they felt that justice had been denied them in the court of their lord. During the days of my worthless nephew, no one had dared appeal to the king, for Stephen was stupid and mean and would decide cases only as they suited him.

Henry knew that he could not force people to appeal their cases to the king's court. They had to want to, so he made his courts very attractive. A man would find fairer treatment in the king's court than at any other. For one thing, Henry used a jury of witnesses. Trial by jury was better than trial by combat or trial by ordeal. What kind of a chance did a man have in a trial by ordeal? Throwing a bound man into a pond of water and claiming him guilty if he floated seemed to me more a matter of the man's habits of eating than his habits with the law.

Everyone began to appeal to the king's court, and Henry had clerks record what happened. When people came with a complaint similar to an earlier one, Henry would check the records and see how the matter had been settled before. In that way everyone received the same treatment under the law, a law common to everyone, the English Common Law.

Henry barely stayed still in those days. He spent as much time in motion as the waters of the ocean, and his roar was as loud. He would tell his court that they should be ready to leave at noon. But if Henry happened to be up at dawn, he would be ready to go that minute, and the whole court would be thrown into a frenzy to make everything ready including several wagons carrying nothing but the parchment rolls on which he had written the decisions of his courts. At other times everything would be ready at sunrise, and Henry would sleep until noon. The entire bailey of the castle would be filled with people dozing and waiting for that loud first call of their king.

Henry dismounted from his horse to sleep, to eat and to pray, but for little else.

"Henry," Eleanor said, "the children think their father is a centaur."

Henry got down on all fours and chased his sons, Henry and Richard, and caught them. He swung them up, one in each arm, then set them upon his knees, left and right. "A centaur is a pagan invention," Henry said to them. "Half man, half horse. I am all Christian and all king," he said.

"Only the king part is divided," Eleanor added. "It is half English, half French."

"Yes," Henry agreed. "This is a nice tight little island, this England, but my lands in France need attention. I am appointing a chancellor to take care of things here while I am off to France."

"Surely Mother Matilda and I can hold . . ."

"Eleanor, I need you with me often. We must often appear together. Especially in Aquitaine where I am still regarded as a foreigner. Besides, you add comfort to my rooms and softness to my manners."

"Who will be your chancellor?" Eleanor asked.

"Becket. Thomas Becket. He is highly recommended. He is energetic and efficient."

"I have heard that he trained as a priest," Eleanor said.

"Yes, but not for the same reasons your Louis did. Louis saw the priesthood as the way to satisfy his ambition to get someplace in Heaven, but Thomas Becket saw the priesthood as a way to satisfy his ambitions to get someplace here on Earth. Louis is a man of lofty birth with plain tastes; Becket is a man of plain birth with high tastes."

Thomas Becket became my son's chancellor, his comrade and his adviser. Becket's home and hospitality became as popular as the royal court. When there was important work or important play, Becket was Henry's first thought. Eleanor often felt left out. Chancellor Thomas Becket was not a simple man.

7

KING LOUIS may have had more thoughts of the Kingdom of Heaven than the Kingdom of France, but he had enough thought left over to want an heir. He married again. This time his choice was Constance of Spain, a girl best described as sweet—an adjective I reserve for women who lack sufficient spirit to cause trouble. Constance presented Louis with a child in the year 1168. We were assembled at Christmas court that year when the subject of Louis's new child came up.

"They call this one Marguerite," I said.

"How clever!" Eleanor said. "I never would have thought to name a daughter of mine after a flower."

"No," Henry said, "I think it best to name our daughters after queens and mothers of kings, so that they have some notion that they are put on Earth for some reason other than smelling sweet and nodding at the sun."

"Marguerite, Marguerite Capet." Eleanor paused a minute and then added, "I've just been thinking, Henry."

"You are always guilty of that, madam," Henry answered.

"If I know Louis," Eleanor said, "and I *do* know Louis, right now he is very concerned about what will happen to his kingdom when he dies. He thinks about death all the time, you know. And if I know Louis, and I *do* know Louis, he would like to have his newest daughter engaged to a young man of property so that when he dies, at least his grandchildren can hold France. Louis will have to offer a dowry with this daughter, a considerable dowry, so that she can be engaged to a man of property, considerable property, a man with a title worthy of a princess of France."

"And you believe that Louis would be interested in a young man of property—considerable property—even if that young man of property has as his father a great rival king?" Henry asked.

"Yes," Eleanor answered. "And even if that young man has as his mother, Louis's own former wife."

Henry thought a minute, but only a minute. "I'll have Becket arrange it," he said. He smiled. "Becket will arrange the engagement of our son Henry to Louis's Marguerite."

"Why Becket?" Eleanor asked. "It was my idea. Besides who knows how to impress Louis's people better than I?"

"No one knows better, my dear," Henry answered.

"But Becket knows as well. And besides, the Franks do not resent Becket, but they do resent you. Louis resents you, too. He has never forgiven you for divorcing him."

"Oh, you're right, Henry. Of course, you're right. It's just that I would love to arrange a great pageant to impress those Franks."

"Becket will do it. He will do a great job. He will make every single bishop, baron, priest, duke, monk, count and serf realize that their former queen is better married than she was."

Eleanor smiled at Henry. "I should say so." She patted her stomach. "And when this little Plantagenet arrives, we shall outmatch them by our three sons to their zero."

"What makes you so certain that you are carrying another boy?"

"I know. I just know. His name will be Geoffrey—after your father."

8

A MODERN CIRCUS train is dusty and fourth rate compared to the parade that Becket arranged to impress the French. He traveled down from Normandy with a caravan that would have been appreciated even in Constantinople. I can only wonder at its effect on people whose lives had no color or sparkle.

Every place they stopped, the men unloaded the chests that contained the gold and silver plate. And everywhere they stopped, they distributed beer, free to all who could make their way to the wagon. When they arrived in Paris, their party was so enormous that there were no quarters large enough to put them up, so they stayed outside the city gates.

What a contrast King Louis was to Thomas Becket. Louis wore a plain monk's cloak, and his manners could not be distinguished from those of a simple priest. He was always opening doors for people—even the lowliest.

Thomas knew as well as Eleanor did that a monarch was often the only touch of glamour and color that peasants had in their lives. Seeing a long-tailed monkey, dressed in bright livery and riding the back of a pack mule, would be something to tell children and grandchildren about. Both Eleanor and Thomas Becket had a social conscience of sorts; they both felt that being grand was their duty. And what a happy coincidence that their duty matched their temperament.

Thomas returned successful. Triumphant. "Louis VII, the King of France, has consented to the betrothal of his six-month-old daughter, Marguerite, to your three-year-old son, Henry," he reported.

"Bravo!" Eleanor replied.

"What will be her dowry?" Henry asked.

"A wedge, a triangle, a corner, a . . ."

"Ah, Thomas, you did it!" Henry went over and clapped Thomas on the back. "You did it!" He turned to Eleanor and said, "We got the Vexin. That little wedge, that little triangle, that my father had to give up. Remember, Eleanor?"

"Of course, I remember, Henry. He gave up the Vexin, and you got the Aquitaine." She looked up and smiled, "And me. Now you have the Vexin returned to you." She looked at Becket as she said, "And that, Henry, is as much due to me as it is due to Becket. I bore you the son who redeemed the Vexin."

"That's true, my queen," Becket answered. "I acted merely as negotiator. But King Louis did have two requests. One, that the castles of the Vexin be held by

The French people thought, "If the Chancellor of the English can afford all this, imagine what the King of the E

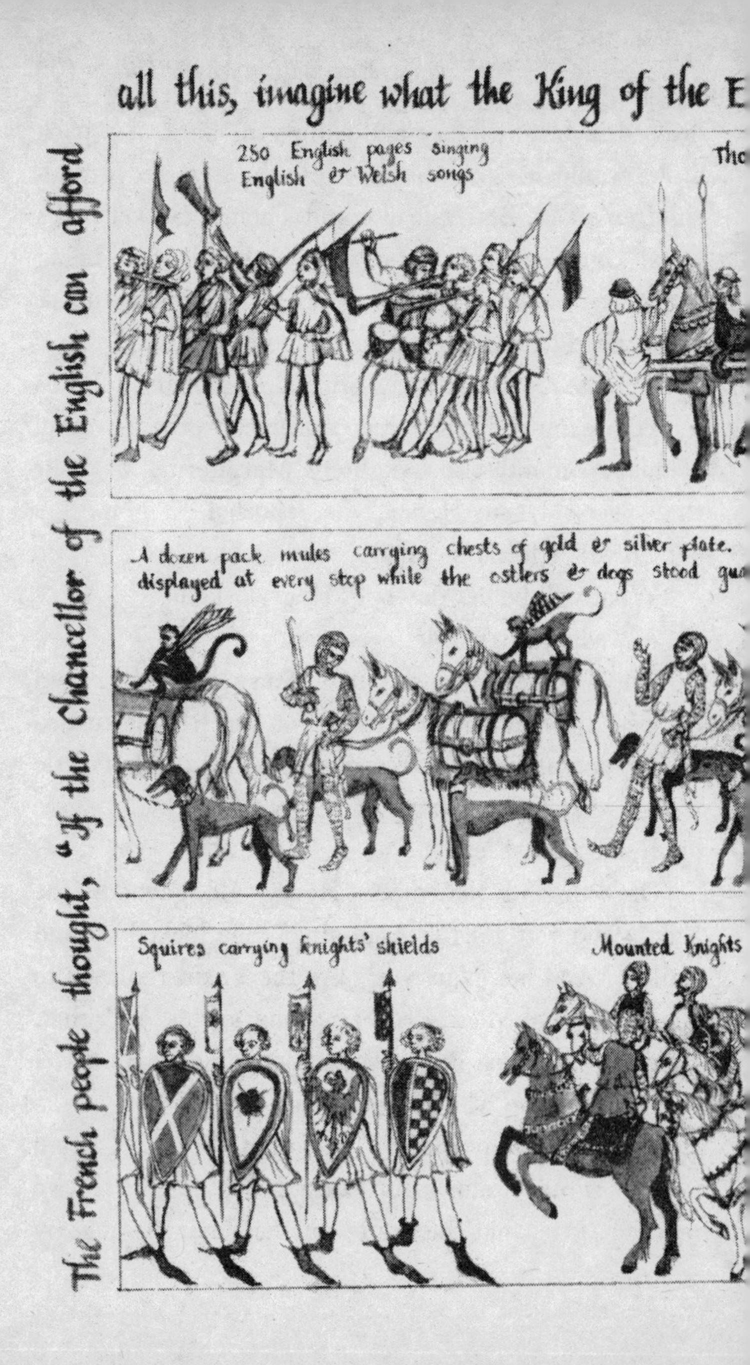
250 English pages singing
English & Welsh songs
Tho
A dozen pack mules carrying chests of gold & silver plate.
displayed at every step while the ostlers & dogs stood gu
Squires carrying knights' shields
Mounted Knights

can afford." And that is exactly what
the King of the English wanted the people of France to think ~
cket's private chapel
Carts with beer & carts with food to give away to the people of France
tents of the chests were
he monkeys entertained.
Grooms & hawkers
The Chancellor Thomas Becket
himself

the Knights Templar, a neutral force, until Henry and Marguerite are married, and," Becket added, looking at his queen, "there was another request."

"Yes?" Eleanor asked. "What was that?"

"You know that it is the custom for a betrothed princess to be reared in the court of her future husband."

"Oh, do I know that!" Eleanor exclaimed. "I was ever grateful to my father that he had never betrothed me as an infant. I would have turned out all wrong if I had been reared anywhere but in the Aquitaine."

Henry laughed. "There are those, madam, who would question what you mean by turning out right."

Eleanor looked at Henry and smiled. "No one who matters questions that I have turned out anything but right."

Becket cleared his throat, "Well . . . about King Louis's request. He will not agree to the match unless he is assured that Marguerite's education and care will be supervised by someone other than Eleanor."

Henry and Becket both looked at Eleanor for a reaction. Eleanor threw her head back and laughed. "Is Louis afraid that I will teach her to sing, or is he afraid that I will teach her to dance, or is he afraid that I'll teach her to use some naughty words in chapel?" Then she looked at Henry and Becket and said, "I am happy to be relieved of the care of sweet Constance's daughter. I had not expected such a bonus in the bargain."

Henry and Becket exchanged a glance. For all her bravado, Eleanor's pride had been hurt.

"You have done your work well, Thomas," Eleanor said. "We seem to excel at the same things, you and I. We both love splendor and show. We both set a fine table. We both are efficient administrators. Now, Thomas, I suggest that you attempt to raise a child." Eleanor turned to Henry and said, "Surely Louis would approve of his daughter's education being in the hands of this man who studied for the priesthood and who charmed him out of the Vexin."

"An excellent idea, Eleanor," Henry said. "Thomas, find some proper teachers and nurses, and you shall be in charge of the young couple."

"Thank you, your majesty," Thomas said. "I hope that I shall do all that is expected of me."

"You always do more," Eleanor replied.

"*More* is what I receive, madam."

"Goodnight, Thomas," Eleanor said.

"Goodnight, Tom," Henry added. "Remember, falconing tomorrow at dawn."

"Speaking of falcons . . ." Thomas added.

"Yes?" Henry asked as he followed his chancellor out the door and left Eleanor alone with me. And with her thoughts.

9

FOR A WHILE it seemed that Eleanor and my son Henry could do nothing wrong, and Louis and Constance could do nothing right. Only two years after the birth of Marguerite, Eleanor came to me with the news that Constance had had another child and that Constance had died at childbirth. Another daughter. They named this one Alais.

"Is Louis in mourning?" I asked.

"*In panic* would better describe him. He is forty years old and the father of four daughters; he has lost two wives, one by design and one by death, and is still without an heir."

"What will he do?" I asked.

"It is not a question of what he will do; it is a question of what he has done. He has remarried already. Less than a month after Constance's death."

"Who is the lucky bride this time?"

"A cousin," Eleanor answered.

"No!" I was genuinely shocked.

"Yes!" Eleanor laughed. "Since Abbot Bernard has

passed away and is not there to shout *cousin!* in his ear, he has married Adele of Champagne."

I smiled. "He apparently likes to keep it all in the family. He betrothed your daughter Marie to one of Adele's brothers, and he betrothed your Alix to another one, and he himself marries Adele. That makes his sons-in-law also his brothers-in-law, and in a sense it makes sisters of his daughters. The complications overwhelm me."

"It is strange to think that when I was married to Louis, he was at war with Champagne. Now both families appear to share a single bed."

"Your daughters are well married," I reassured her. "Take comfort. The House of Champagne is powerful and rich."

"My beautiful Marie is engaged to Henry, Henry of Champagne; she is fifteen, he is twice that. She will be married to a rich *old* man."

"You seem to care nothing about a difference in age when the lady is the senior and the man is the junior."

Eleanor laughed. "We both seem to have a shaded point of view about that."

"What does Henry intend to do now that Louis is married again?"

"He has decided that we should marry Young Henry to Marguerite immediately. The Vexin must be ours. If this new wife of Louis's, this Adele, presents Louis with a son, Louis will find that he has not enough land or enough wealth to divide it with the Plantagenets."

"Has Henry found a priest who will perform the ceremony?"

"Certainly he has. All will be done in accordance with the law. You know that Henry has more respect for the law than he has for promises. That is why he is insisting on this marriage. As long as Marguerite and Henry are only engaged, the Vexin is only a Capet's promise to a Plantagenet. As soon as they are married, Marguerite and the Vexin are legally ours."

"And then?" I asked.

"And then after the young couple is married, Henry will dismiss the Templars from the Vexin and take over its fortresses. Since Young Henry is but five and Marguerite is but two, you stand no chance of being rushed into great-grandmotherhood. After the marriage the children will be returned to their nursery to finish growing up."

"Speaking of their growing up, how is Thomas Becket, Eleanor?"

"He is as beautiful as ever, Mother Matilda. He does well whatever task is asked of him. If he had been born a cow, he would have spurted pure cream."

"I see you care for him as little as ever."

"I would like him more if Henry liked him less."

10

I ARRANGED TO ATTEND Easter court in France to help Eleanor and Henry celebrate ten years of marriage. Ten very successful years.

Henry called Thomas to France, too.

Henry, being a great believer in having people renew their oaths of allegiance, wanted Thomas to convene court in London. He wanted all the barons and the bishops of England to pledge support to Young Henry to remind them that when he passed from the scene, there was another Henry Plantagenet waiting.

"Buy him a little crown and some royal robes; it will help remind the English that he is a future king. And, Thomas, I want you as my chancellor to be the first to kneel and pay homage."

Thomas Becket answered, "I consider it an honor to pay homage to so young and fair a prince. And I shall be happy to be the first to do so. But the homage paid by the king's chancellor weighs as a penny to a pound compared to the importance of the homage paid by the Archbishop of Canterbury."

"But there is no Archbishop of Canterbury at the moment. You know, that, Tom. Thibault died several months ago, and the Pope has not yet chosen someone to take his place."

"That is true, sire," Thomas Becket said. "Too bad. But I shall be happy to be the first to kneel to Young Henry."

Henry smiled. "Tom, what if . . . what if . . . the Archbishop of Canterbury and my chancellor were one and the same person?"

"Oh, I am flattered, my king. But a man cannot wear two hats at the same time."

"Don't be ridiculous," Henry said. "If I can wear two crowns, surely you can wear two hats. Think about it, Thomas."

Thomas said, "My taste in hats is too fancy for a bishop's miter, my lord."

"Tastes change." Henry smiled.

Thomas bowed and left the room. He was no sooner gone than Eleanor and I both pounced on Henry.

Eleanor first. "What makes you think, dear husband, that you will be able to appoint Thomas as bishop. The Pope guards his right to appoint all bishops, and he certainly will not allow you to appoint one as important as the Archbishop of Canterbury. The Archbishop of Canterbury is the Pope's eye in England. My former husband, Louis, once tried to appoint only some minor bishops, and it brought nothing but trouble. He lost the bishops and considerable prestige."

Henry answered, "Your former husband, your Louis,

did not work *within* the law. I shall. I shall only *suggest* to a few important people that Thomas Becket be named Archbishop of Canterbury."

"Suggest to some and bribe others. Is that it, Henry?" I asked.

"Oh, Mother, don't call it bribery. Call it an exchange. Why don't you like the idea?"

"Because it will not work. Becket will make a choice. He is a man of conscience. I see that by how conscientiously he serves you as chancellor. He will choose to serve God instead of you. If you make him archbishop, you give him too much power and too hard a choice."

"Out. Out. Out. Both of you. You, you women! Your brains are . . . "

Eleanor and I were quite accustomed to Henry's rages. We stood our ground. Eleanor said, "I will not get out, Henry. I will stand here and stand opposed to your appointing Becket as Archbishop of Canterbury."

Henry walked over to Eleanor, picked her up from the waist and deposited her on his chair. She looked up, "You see, Henry, even *I* like your throne. It gives the best point of view by far. Can you imagine Becket not wanting to set his fancy bottom on such a fancy seat?"

Henry had to laugh. Laughter quieted his anger. "All right, ladies," he said, "I'll explain. Mother sit here, in Eleanor's chair. Eleanor, stay there. Let me explain. Now listen. All the times I have not had to go to war, I have spent my time developing the law of this land. I have made the English law firm and just and uniform throughout the island. Except for one thing. And that is the Church. Anyone who claims that he is the lowliest clerk in the tiniest church is excused from English law and is allowed to be tried by Church law. Let me give you an example. A wool merchant in London accused a boy of stealing a bale of wool. The boy said that he did not steal the wool at all; he said that the merchant had counted wrong. The merchant replied that he had not counted wrong at all and that the boy was lying. Without any further investigation, the merchant had the young man's tongue cut out."

Eleanor winced. Henry continued, "He said that the boy would never lie again. The mother of the boy came to my court. She wanted a trial by jury. She could produce witnesses, she said, that would prove that the bales had not been counted correctly. I was ready to call a trial when I was visited by none other than the merchant's bishop. 'You cannot try the merchant in your court,' he said. 'Since he is a member of the clergy, he must be tried by the officers of the Church, not the officers of the king's court.' So the merchant was tried by a Church court and found not guilty. The Church may preach an eye for an eye, but not a tongue for a tongue."

"Could you not prove that the merchant was not a member of the clergy?" I asked.

Henry laughed. A loud guffaw. "Do you know what it takes to prove that you are clergy, Mother? It takes nothing more than being able to recite six verses from the Bible by heart. They are called *neck verses* because they've saved many a neck. But, of course, if you are a young lad who has had his tongue cut out, you can't recite verses."

Eleanor and I stayed silent. Henry paced around the room, frowning at everything. Then he stood between our two chairs and rested one hand on each. He leaned over and said, very solemnly, "You see now, ladies, why I must have Becket as Archbishop of Canterbury as well as chancellor. The country cannot have two kinds of laws. One set of laws for the king's men and another set of laws for the Church's men. I must combine them. What if men were different colors? Would it be right to have one set of laws for blue men and another set for red? Good grief! ladies, what can I do to convince you that I must have one set of laws in all my kingdom?" Henry was raging again.

"You've convinced us, Henry," I said. "I do not question the wisdom of your wants, I question the way. Find someone else to be Archbishop of Canterbury, someone else who will listen to you."

"Mother, Mother! Don't you know Thomas? He loves splendor as much as my wife does. He is not about to quit wearing brocade. By making Becket Archbishop of Canterbury, I am saving myself the trouble of finding another friend at court."

"You will not save trouble," I warned. "You will buy it."

"Look at Louis, my former husband," Eleanor said. "He cannot make up his mind whether he wants to be mighty king or a lowly priest. So he does neither well."

"*That* will not be Thomas's problem," I said. "Thomas will do whatever job is set before him, and he will do it well. Too well. He will always give his best to the higher sovereign. And, Henry, my son, as much as I love you, you are no match for God. Thomas will choose to serve God rather than you."

Henry's calm broke again. "One of you compares me to a sissy king and the other to God on high. Now, just for a moment, as a husband to one of you and as a son to the other, for just a moment, think of me as your king." He paused, smiled, then said, "Are you doing that, both of you?"

We nodded.

"Are you thinking of me as your king?"

We nodded again.

Henry smiled again. "Then your king orders you *out*, *out!* OUT! OUT!"

We left.

Henry kicked the door closed behind us.

11

AND SO IT WAS. The world well knows the story of the feud that developed between my son, King Henry, and his Archbishop, Thomas Becket.

Shortly after he was named Archbishop of Canterbury, Becket resigned as chancellor. Henry went into a rage and removed Young Henry and Marguerite from Becket's care. He tried to get Becket to sign an agreement that made it illegal for clergy to stand trial in courts different from the laymen's. Becket would not sign, and the private quarrel that began between Henry and Thomas Becket became public.

I was right. Becket chose to serve God.

He cast away his fine robes and wore a monk's robe. The man who had worn hose of silk now walked barefoot, and there were people who said that he wore a hair shirt as a constant itch to his conscience. Just as Becket had been popular with lords and barons when he was chancellor, he was now popular with the common folk. They followed him through Canterbury like the children of Israel following Moses to the Promised Land.

Henry's hopes for uniting the two kinds of law were

dashed. He fumed, he raged, he shouted to the world. Henry claimed that Becket was in contempt of the king's court; he called Becket before him and issued heavy fines. Still Becket would not sign the agreement. Henry accused; Becket refused.

The war between the two men soon became a war between the country and the Church, and Becket fled. He sought shelter with King Louis of France, and he found it.

Henry dissolved into another rage. "If Louis wants some Becket," Henry shouted, "he shall have a flood of Beckets," and Henry banished from England everyone who was even remotely related to his old friend Thomas. France found itself with four hundred relatives of Becket, most of them poor.

In the year after Becket fled from England, my daughter-in-law, Eleanor, gave birth to a daughter; she and Henry named her Joanna. That year, however, is better remembered for another birth.

Louis VII of France at last had a son. He named him Philip Augustus. Louis and his wife Adele were overjoyed.

Henry and his wife Eleanor were not.

12

WE WERE ALL TOGETHER for Easter court the following year. Henry seemed weary and preoccupied; he claimed he was exhausted from just having waged battle in Wales. Eleanor looked weary and pregnant. I was weary and old. It was a tired court that year.

In the fall, Henry and I stayed in France, and Eleanor crossed the Channel to England. In December, Eleanor gave birth to John, and shortly thereafter she returned to France. I heard that Eleanor was on her way to Poitiers, and I sent word that I wished her to stop in and see me on the way. I wanted to bid my newest grandson welcome. When a person reaches the age I then was, there are many more goodbyes than hellos. The *hellos* become precious.

Eleanor came. She did not stay long. She said that she was anxious to get her family to the Aquitaine for the winter. She complained of a chill. In the fifteen years that I had known Eleanor, I had never heard her complain of discomfort. The cold that she felt was something inside, I was sure. But she would not talk of it.

I died shortly after that visit, and I still don't know what drove Eleanor South, home to the Aquitaine.

Back in Heaven

ELEANOR REACHED across her mother-in-law's lap and took her hand. "There are some things, Mother Matilda, that wives have to find out, and mothers never should."

"At least tell me what happened to Thomas while he remained on Earth."

"He stayed in France for six years. Then he returned to England and was murdered. People blamed Henry for Becket's murder. Young Henry blamed him more than anyone else; after all, Thomas had been as much a father to him as Henry had been. I think that Becket's murder was the single act that has most delayed Henry's coming Up. Henry did not wish it; while he was overcome with one of his rages, he screamed, 'Won't anyone rid me of this troublesome clerk?' Someone is always willing to oblige a king. Four of Henry's knights made their way to Canterbury and murdered Becket while he was at prayer in his own cathedral."

"Did Becket ever come Up?" Matilda-Empress asked.

"Oh, immediately," Eleanor answered.

"Why then do I never see him?"

"Because, my dear mother-in-law, he became a Saint. He is St. Thomas Becket now. Even though Saints are supposed to be something between men and Angels, they always stay closer to the Angels. He still serves the higher sovereign, just as you said he would."

Abbot Suger interrupted. "Too bad it was left for a different Henry to make the Church give up the right to try its clergy," he said. "Henry the Eighth did that. Three hundred fifty years after Becket's murder. That Henry took everything: the courts, the Church treasures, the land belonging to the monasteries. I had arrived Up long before Henry VIII's break with the Church. I watched the whole thing happen. I've always kept up my interest in Church matters. It was said that when Henry VIII took over the Church of England, all Hell broke loose. I am surprised you didn't hear the rumble, Matilda-Empress."

Matilda-Empress did not enjoy being reminded about her dark years Below. "It seems to me, dear Suger, that the same thing happened in France, too. I was Up by the time it happened there. I watched your beautiful church at St. Denis being destroyed by the French people during the French Revolution. I saw them tear down the gold cross of which you were so proud; they knocked the heads off your precious statues, and they made dust of your stained glass. They especially hated St. Denis because your French kings were buried there, and the time of kings was past. It seems to me, Abbot, that the French created quite a roar in Heaven, but I never bothered to find out if *that* rumble reached Hell. Fortunately, I don't have that kind of morbid curiosity."

Abbot Suger lowered his eyes and nodded his head slowly.

Eleanor put her arm around the little monk's shoulder. "I remember, Abbot. Those were the days you cried in Heaven. I remember."

"Sh, sh," the Abbot whispered. "In Heaven, one is not supposed to care for worldly things. About a century ago they tried to piece my church back together, but, like Humpty Dumpty, it can't be put back together again. Once something is broken, it is hard to repair it so that the damage doesn't show. That happens with friendships, too."

"And also with marriages," said William the Marshal. "We seem to have strayed from the subject of Queen Eleanor."

"To switch from talk of Eleanor to talk of the Church is to have strayed indeed," said Eleanor, laughing. "But leave it to a noble knight to not forget his purpose."

"Well, I'm glad you're here to bring us back to Eleanor," Matilda-Empress said.

William the Marshal replied, "I would be most happy to continue the story of Queen Eleanor. That is, if she does not mind."

Eleanor waved her arm and said, "Tell anything you want to."

"I want, my lady, to tell only the truth."

"Ah, yes! The true and noble knight will tell only the true and noble truth. Come, sit, William. Sit and spin your tale."

"You might say, my lady, that I shall weave my tale but not embroider it."

"William!" Eleanor exclaimed, "to find wit in you is to make me believe that in Heaven all things are truly possible."

William the Marshal's Tale
Part Three

1

QUEEN ELEANOR went South for two reasons. One reason was that King Henry wanted her to. He had recently quieted some rebellions in the Aquitaine, but the peace there was touchy. He hoped that by sending his wife there, the people would stay quiet. The people of the South, he thought, would respond better to one of their own kind. That was the king's reason.

The other reason for Queen Eleanor's going South was that she wanted to, and for the first time in fifteen years her reason was not the same as her husband's. Queen Eleanor's reason for leaving England was Rosamond, Rosamond Clifford.

Rosamond Clifford was the girl King Henry had met and fallen in love with while he was fighting in Wales. The queen did not choose to stay in a country where she was number two.

Queen Eleanor had found out about Rosamond when John was about to be born and she had gone to Oxford for her lying-in. She had heard the name *Rosamond* whispered about. Seeing young ladies throw themselves at Henry was simply seeing something that happened to kings, and something that queens learned to put up with. Queen Eleanor had joked about these ladies at court; she called them "Henry's Harem." But to hear a name whispered instead of spoken out loud made the queen suspicious. She investigated; she went to Woodstock, not far from Oxford, and there she saw Rosamond.

Queen Eleanor took no revenge upon her rival. Rosamond was not to blame. What young girl could resist a king? Especially Henry. Queen Eleanor never mentioned Rosamond to Henry either. She never accused him. She never asked him to admit or deny. She knew what she would do. She would return to her native Aquitaine, and there she would set up court, and there she would rear her sons to manhood. And to rebellion.

I had just been made a knight when I was sent by King Henry to accompany Queen Eleanor to Poitiers. The lords of the Aquitaine were waiting for a chance for revenge. Just outside of Poitiers, they ambushed us. It was my first chance to prove myself as a knight. My horse was killed from under me, but I put my back against a hedge and warded off all who came until I knew that my queen was safely inside the castle.

I was wounded, and I was captured, but my bravery did not go unnoticed. Queen Eleanor herself paid my ransom. I went to the castle to thank her for her generosity, and she rewarded me further. She gave me a horse, arms and clothing. She also gave me my first job; I was made knight-at-arms to the royal children.

That was the beginning of my remarkable rise in the royal household and in the world. Through loyalty and devotion to the Plantagenets, I became a wealthy and famous man. During my service to the royal family, I had to switch loyalties to stay on the same side—the side of truth and justice. My devotion sometimes had to change direction, but it never changed degree; I was always completely loyal and true.

2

QUEEN ELEANOR was a generous ruler and hostess. Her court at Poitiers was open to everyone, and everyone came. Poets and troubadours came; cousins came, dozens of cousins from the Aquitaine who were happy to have a headquarters again. Second sons of famous dukes and barons came; they had no money and no skills. Besides these cousins and second sons, there were the queen's own children, seven in all, plus the girls her sons were to marry. The castle at Poitiers was nursery, home, school and seat of government. Children and adolescents were aswarming. The air in the bailey was fetid with the scent of overactive glands. For all of these young people had two things in common: too much time and not enough responsibility.

Life in Poitiers was boisterous. For example, one day at dinner, Young Henry and his friends rode their horses straight into the dining hall, a pack of hounds at their heels. They began to eat while still mounted. Queen Eleanor continued eating. She looked up casually and said, "My duties as queen occasionally demand that I sup with a horse's ass, but I have never been asked to dine with the horse itself. And I shall not. You may leave this dining hall, Henry. You may leave it right now, and you may not return until after you have dismounted and washed."

After that incident Queen Eleanor was determined that her court should be gay but quiet enough to give her some peace while she was conducting the affairs of state. She wanted her court to be like Constantinople but more vigorous. She needed help to do that. So she sent for Marie, her very first child, the one she had borne when she had been a Capet, the daughter that she and Louis had hoped would be a boy. Marie was now married to Henry of Champagne and was the mother of two children herself. King Louis had married the sister of Henry of Champagne. That made King Louis not only father-in-law but also brother-in-law to Henry of Champagne. Over and above all this, he was his overlord. Thus, as father, brother and as king, he urged Henry of Champagne to allow his wife to join Queen Eleanor's court at Poitiers and tidy it up. King Louis wanted Marie to keep an eye on his other daughter, Marguerite, the princess who had been married to Young Henry.

Marie had her mother's gift of using the materials at hand. What were those materials? I repeat: poets, troubadours, adolescents, time, high spirits and noise. Marie of Champagne decided that the ingredients were good, but the proportions were not. To rearrange the elements and to hold them all together, she knew she needed a common cause, something that was uppermost in everyone's mind. She chose love.

The poets were given old legends of battles and heroes and told to rewrite them, putting the emphasis on love. The troubadours were paid for writing songs in praise of women and love. And then Marie organized the whole castle into an elaborate game called the Courts of Love.

The Courts of Love had laws: the male must be polite, he must be neat, he must regard his lady-love as someone above earthly temptation, as someone too frail to be exposed to the roughness of life, as someone to protect, as someone who must be helped to sit at table, as someone whose delicate ears must not hear naughty words, as someone to tip one's hat to.

Young knights would bring their cases before a court, which was made up of young ladies. They would tell of their love for the lady, someone worshiped from afar, someone who often was already married. A knight would tell his story, and fellow knights would testify to the man's behavior and to his sincerity. The jury would read from the book of Rules of Courtly Love. Penalties—some songs or some poems or being pelted by roses—were given. The judgments of the Courts of Love were recorded like the English Common Law.

The Courts of Love were a great success; they quieted the riotous behavior in Poitiers then, and they are still responsible for the fact that men open doors for ladies and stand when a lady walks into a room.

Until the inventions of Queen Eleanor and Marie of Champagne, women were considered nothing but property. Marie lifted women out of that; it was she who put them on a pedestal. As chess was a game of war, the courts were a game of love, but more than two people could play. The whole bailey could play. Each society invents a game about a part of life it takes seriously. I sometimes look down now and see children playing Monopoly, a game of business.

I managed another activity that kept the young men busy. That was the tournaments. Young Henry was the idol of the tournament crowd. Small wonder. He was clever, and he was lovable. He was generous, and he was easy to bring to laughter. I will give two examples.

One day as we were riding to a tournament, we stopped to refresh ourselves by a spring. As we dismounted, thirsty and dusty, we discovered that there was only one bottle of wine among us. We numbered forty-two. The single bottle belonged to Young Henry. "I shall share it," he said. He emptied the bottle into the spring. "Diluted, but equal," he said, laughing.

On another occasion we were riding through

Normandy, and I mentioned to him that it was my birthday.

"Your birthday, William? You should not celebrate alone."

"I am not alone, my prince. I keep company with the best of men, and any time with you is marked as a celebration."

"Thank you. I, too, consider myself in good company when I am with a William. I think I should like to dine with many Williams." He called for a page and ordered him to round up every William in town. William was the second most common name in Normandy, the Normans still being proud to name children for their hero, William the Conqueror. One hundred ten Williams came to dine. Young Henry saw to it that each had a good time. With him as host, and with me as guest of honor, how could they not?

There were only two things wrong with the tournaments. They were expensive, and they fostered jealousy between the brothers, Henry and Richard.

Richard was actually better than Henry at combat, but he took his losses too seriously. Henry preferred to win, but he liked participating as much as he liked winning. Henry would lose, and the winner, as was his right, would hold Henry and his horse for ransom. Henry made an art of the bargaining. Richard would not. Henry developed his wit to deal with people as

Richard sharpened his sword. Richard was not a boy altogether without wit. When he became a man, he wrote poetry, some very fine poetry, but Richard was without spontaneity. The two sons, Richard and Henry, would have made a perfect team, but as often happens with brothers, each disliked the other for his best qualities.

The jealousy between them came to a climax years later. I was there to witness the end of it as I was there to witness its beginning.

At this point in my career, I was promoted to master-at-arms for my skills and my services.

3

ONCE MARIE OF CHAMPAGNE had settled the children, Queen Eleanor devoted herself to keeping peace in her lands. She knew that it was important to tie up the wounds that years of petty warfare had left, and the queen had learned valuable lessons in government from her years in England.

Politics also kept King Henry busy. He wanted to make certain that the empire that he was putting together would stay in Plantagenet hands. With this purpose in mind, he called his three oldest sons to a meeting with King Louis. The three boys were to pay homage from the lands that had been given them at birth. By paying homage for their lands, the king of France became their overlord and officially recognized their right to inherit the land.

Tall, blond Young Henry knelt first to King Louis and received the kiss of peace. Next was Richard, the broad, strong prince with hair the color of candlelight. Geoffrey, slighter and quieter than his brothers, did the same. The Plantagenet princes were a handsome trio, and King Louis was pleased to recognize their right to the lands of Normandy, Anjou, the Aquitaine and Brittany.

John was too young to share in the inheritance. Poor John. King Henry nicknamed him John Lackland, and then he went about conquering Ireland for him.

Queen Eleanor introduced Richard, who was to have the Aquitaine, to her people. Richard traveled with his mother wherever she went. He took part in every ceremony. He sat by his mother when she held court and when she collected taxes. He learned everything about government at her side.

Young Henry was supposed to learn government from his father, but King Henry was a different kind of teacher. After he had finished conquering Ireland (for John), he had Young Henry accompany him as he traveled throughout England. But the jobs he gave Young Henry were more those of an errand boy than those of a prince. I was often in the difficult position of trying to explain the father to the son. And vice versa.

Young Henry would tire of the jobs he was given, and he would complain to his father. King Henry would not sympathize. "Every job in the world has some built-in boredom. No man can stay excited about something every minute he is doing it. Routine is as necessary to life as water is to beer; it is the base that holds the flavors and spices together."

Young Henry saw how his mother taught Richard the ways of the Aquitaine, how she allowed him to make decisions as well as to do the routine, and his anger at his father grew. He went on a feverish round of tournaments. He became careless and then reckless.

King Henry wanted to curb the expenses of the tournaments, and he tried to lure Young Henry back with gifts and other bribes. Young Henry would not be tempted. Then the king offered his son the crown of England.

"To be king means to be no man's vassal," Young Henry said to me. "Not even my father's."

I knew that the crown that Young Henry would wear would mean no more than his titles to Normandy and Anjou. But I said nothing. A master-at-arms must also be a master-at-tact.

Queen Eleanor helped to plan the coronation ceremony; she made certain that it was elegant. Having her son crowned King of England fit well into her plan to breed a rebellion of all of her sons against their father. Since the coronation was held in England, the queen chose not to attend.

At the banquet following the ceremony, King Henry himself carried the tray that held the roast pig to the table. "Is it not a great honor to have a prince served by a king?" I remarked to Young Henry.

Young Henry looked at his father and answered, "It is surely no great honor to have the son of a king served by the son of a count."

The situation between father and son got worse after the coronation. Young Henry's jobs remained the same, but they seemed less for his titles had become more.

4

BY THE TIME the Plantagenets held Christmas court in 1172, Queen Eleanor had had six years to train her sons in chivalry and in rebellion. After all the official holiday ceremonies were over, the family found itself together, and the topic of John came up.

John was now six years old, and he was already a difficult child to like. John had unkind opinions about everything and everyone, and he told them at the top of his voice. John's natural expression was a scowl. John cheated at games, and John told lies. It was impossible for most people to like John, but King Henry loved him. He loved him beyond reason, but then, all love is beyond reason.

When his name came up for discussion that Christmas, John smiled for the first time in two days. There was something unlovely even about his smile; it was so smug that it was a challenge not to punch him. I reminded myself that a noble knight does not hit those who are younger than he.

King Henry started the discussion. "Eleanor, dear," he began, "our little boy John is very much on my mind. Our girls are all well spoken for, our older sons all have a good portion, but poor little John has nothing. Little John Lackland." John smiled at his father and rested his head in his father's lap.

Richard was annoyed. He cared as little for John as he did for Henry. Geoffrey was the only one of his brothers who did not annoy him. Geoffrey was businesslike and kept to himself. Richard looked at John, and his annoyance swelled. "Wipe your nose, John," he said.

John walked over to his brother and wiped his nose on Richard's sleeve. Richard lifted his arm to hit him, but the king stopped him. He laughed; he picked John up and put him on his knee. "I like a boy who immediately does as he is told," he said. He looked at his older boys. "I want each of us to give John a little something." King Henry unrolled a map and pointed. "There is a spot where Anjou, which is Henry's, meets Poitou which is Richard's and also touches Brittany which is Geoffrey's. I think that we should all pitch in and give John a castle, one castle apiece." He pointed out the castles: one, two, three. "Poor John," he added, "needs something so that I can arrange some kind of marriage for him."

Now Young Henry's temper flared. "You have gotten Ireland for this snot-nose. That is enough."

"But, Henry, my son, we want to marry John to

someone of worth. What good is marriage if it doesn't extend the empire?"

Queen Eleanor looked up at that. "Some marriages unite people as well as territories."

King Henry ignored her remark. "No one worthwhile will have John if he has only Ireland. Ireland is practically pagan. The people there dance naked in the woods on Midsummer Eve."

"Oh, that would never do for John," Young Henry said, "hopping around naked like that, people might mistake him for a pimpled toad and cook him up into a potion. But I wouldn't worry about John, Father. John will find a way to marry and get land. He is already a capable liar and a wonderful cheat. What he cannot gain honestly, he will take without honor."

King Henry rolled the map up. He smiled and reached his arm across Young Henry's shoulder, "Henry, my son, I may as well tell you. I have already promised those castles as well as a few estates in England to a very rich count who happens to have a very marriageable daughter."

"A few estates in England. England! Again you see a way to clip my feathers."

"Ah, my boy, what are a few pinfeathers to a bird of such fine plumage?"

"Yes, Father," Richard interrupted, "we all have fine

plumage. Bright plumage, but it is purely ornamental. When will you let us fly?"

"Never," Queen Eleanor answered. "Your father expects you to stay in the nest forever, my sons." Then she looked at her husband and said, "Those are not your castles or your estates to give, my husband. Young Henry has been crowned and recognized by the people of England as their king, and Richard, Geoffrey and Henry have paid homage for their territories in France. Henry, my husband, you may give Ireland to John, but I'm afraid that you have no right to give him anything else."

King Henry turned on her. "I have every right! I built the nest. Those castles and estates are mine. I have fought to keep this land together. I now have a chance of marrying John to a princess." Henry came over to Eleanor and spoke directly to her. "Don't you see, Eleanor? We can extend our lands all the way to Italy. What has Young Henry done to keep these lands? He does nothing but play at tournaments and at elaborate games of love in your court at Poitiers."

Young Henry was furious. "When have you ever let me do anything that would show you that I can rule? Mother has let Richard rule the Aquitaine with her. They truly share the work. He mashes rebellion with a hammer, and she follows in his wake and passes out bandages. Mother has convinced the people of the Aquitaine that her father, their beloved Duke William, has come to life again in the person of your son, Richard. The Aquitaine is better off without you, Father. Are you afraid that the people of Normandy, Anjou and England will find me a better overlord than you? Is that why you won't let me do anything more than show my face once here and once there and then only to collect your taxes? Is that why you have to chop up my inheritance?"

Queen Eleanor spoke again. She was calm, controlled. "That is only part of the reason, children. Your father will not let you rule because he considers himself the grandest puppeteer in Europe. He believes that for a great performance, he needs only a few puppets and one very large stage—say from Scotland to the Pyrenees and a little bit eastward—say to Italy. That will do for the present. What your father does not realize, children, is that someone, not him, but someone, has put some guts into his puppets. Guts bleed, my husband. Look well. You have just drawn the first blood."

Then Queen Eleanor left the room. Her sons followed. The queen had at last what she had wanted: two sons unwilling to give up the taste of power they had and another one fighting mad to get it. John was nothing in this first rebellion, nothing except the excuse for it.

5

WAR FOLLOWED. Father against son. Father won. King Henry finished his battles with his sons and headed for Poitiers. He knew now that his queen had cost him a war and his son's loyalty. He was hell-bent for a show down. Queen Eleanor was not in Poitiers when he arrived. His fury grew. "Eleanor! Eleanor!" he shouted in the empty halls. Where was that woman?

The truth was that Queen Eleanor was dressed as a knight and was riding toward the borders of France. Some of the king's men were on a routine mission when they chanced upon a small band of knights close to the borders of the land of King Louis. They asked the knights the nature of their business. "Our business is none of yours," answered one of the knights.

"Whatever happens within these borders is our business. We are the men of King Henry, and this land is his."

"You are wrong. This land belongs to his wife," answered the same knight.

One of the guards said to another, "Only a very young knight or an old lady could have so brazen a tongue and so high a voice." Saying that, he pulled the cap from the head of the saucy knight and found that the head with the quick tongue belonged to a lady. More than a lady. It belonged to a queen. Eleanor.

She was taken to the king. The king looked at his wife and asked, "Was it you, Eleanor? Was it you who inspired the rebellion of my sons?"

"Yes, Henry, it was."

The king nodded his head. "I thought as much. Were you going to Louis when you were captured?"

"Yes, Henry, I was."

"You are without shame."

"I am not. A woman without shame has no pride, and I have plenty of that. Pride drove me out of England. Louis is still my overlord. I always say, Henry, that politics makes nicer bedfellows than marriage. Speaking of marriage, Henry, why don't you divorce me? You have excellent grounds. There are no better grounds for divorce than treason."

"No, madam," King Henry answered. "I shall not divorce you and set you free to marry someone else and then sue me for the return of the Aquitaine. There are other remedies for treason, my queen."

"Prison! Are you going to put me in jail, Henry?"

"Call it *house arrest*, madam." King Henry looked at

his wife and saw her smile. "Why do you smile, madam? Don't you fear being my prisoner?"

"Fear is not something I am familiar with, Henry. *Loathing* is. I know that I shall loathe prison more than I shall fear it."

"Why, then, do you smile?"

"Because, Henry, I know that I shall love that loathing, and that spark of love will keep me well."

The queen was taken to England. Henry wanted her far away from him and his sons while he negotiated peace with them. The Channel was high, and the wind was strong when they set sail. Just twenty years before they had made a similar stormy crossing, but that crossing had marked a union and a beginning. This crossing marked a separation and an end. King Henry again stood up in the boat, and he again thrust his fist at the storm. "Hear me, Lord?" he shouted, "see us safely through to the other side of the Channel. Let my will be done upon this woman before Thy will be done."

"Amen," the queen said.

King Henry looked at his wife and roared, "Why are you smiling now, madam?"

"You and my father are the only men I have ever known who grab God by the throat instead of whispering into His good ear," she answered.

"One must get His attention first, madam," Henry said, smiling.

And there, for that moment, the sound of their shared laughter broke through the noise of the storm and the sea.

6

QUEEN ELEANOR was taken to Salisbury. She was allowed to ride in the country, but she was always under guard. She sometimes moved from one castle to another after she had received permission to do so. That, too, was done under guard. She was deprived of the company of her children, and she was deprived of being at the center of affairs. She was deprived of learning of events firsthand and of being the cause of those events.

Not far from Salisbury was the circle of giant stones, called *Stonehenge*. Queen Eleanor loved to ride there and watch the light peek through the openings of the arches made by the stones. The tallest stones were set in an odd pattern of arches, the space between them was too narrow for a horse and rider to pass through.

One day shortly after I had been promoted to marshal, I came to deliver a message. Upon arriving at Salisbury Tower, I was told that the queen had gone to Stonehenge. I rode there to meet her, and I found her sitting astride her horse beside one of the large stones outside the circle.

"My queen seems lost in thought," I said.

"Lost in time," she answered. "Now that the present is denied me, I wonder about the past. I wonder how these stones got here. I ride here often and wonder. Surely these giants are not native to this flat pancake of land."

"It is said, my lady, that Merlin brought these stones from Ireland."

"Merlin who? And who says?"

"Merlin the magician, the teacher of King Arthur. And Geoffrey Monmouth says. Geoffrey of Monmouth wrote a book called the *Histories of the Kings of Britain;* it tells the story of Merlin and King Arthur."

"I want a copy of that book," the queen said.

I promised the queen that she would have a copy of the book before my next visit, and I kept my promise true.

Queen Eleanor did with those histories as she did with everything—she transformed them. She found them interesting, but plain. She thought that they could be improved. Especially the history of King Arthur. She called for her poets and her troubadours; she asked each of them to read the stories and to rewrite them. She asked her writers to dress them up. She suggested that King Arthur's knights be more noble, that the ladies of the court be more fair, that the manners of the whole court be more courtly, like Poitiers. The work of her poets became popular; people from France to Constantinople began to read and to write of Merlin and of the knights of Arthur's court. Galahad, Lancelot, and the traitorous Mordred were lifted from the plain pages of a history book and wrapped around with magic and adventure and romance. And that is how people read of them today. All elegantly clothed in honor and seated at a Round Table in Camelot.

Had I not brought Queen Eleanor that book, King Arthur would have stayed dust bound between Geoffrey of Monmouth's pages, and the people of England would never have had the proud sense of history they have today.

7

MEANWHILE KING HENRY made peace with his sons, giving them little more than they had before except promises; he gave them promises in ever greater numbers. The king continued to be busy with the government of England. He asked Young Henry to join him, and Young Henry did for a while. But I saw the son grow first restless and then bored. The second rebellion began to simmer from the leftover heat of the first.

"I am tired, Father, of being your errand boy. I want something besides titles. I want a court of my own. I have a wife, a queen, and a crown that says that I am King of England, and still I must ask you for spending money. I can do nothing without your knowing. You hold me now, not with puppet strings, but with purse strings. Geoffrey rules Brittany with Constance at his side. Richard rules the Aquitaine like an ill wind, and I haven't even a castle in which I can hold court with men who answer to me instead of to you."

"Being a king is a business," King Henry replied. "It is a lot of privilege, but you pay heavily for that privilege. A king is not a free man."

"I know, sir. You have told me that often. But must I remind you that any king is more free than a queen, a certain queen, at least."

The king was anxious to change that subject. He unrolled a map. "Pick a castle," he said. "You shall have any castle you want, plus a staff, plus a generous allowance for you and Marguerite."

Young Henry chose a castle in Anjou, but after the excitement of setting up was finished, he once again found himself with little to do. All of his friends from his days in Poitiers made their way to his court. They began to call him "Lord of Little Land." Young Henry's best defense was to make people love him. If he could not have their respect, he could have their love. So the tournaments began again. With increased splendor and with increased expense. Young Henry was the leader of the pack.

While Richard was putting down rebellions in the Aquitaine and Geoffrey kept a businesslike kind of order in Brittany, Young Henry was concerned with bargaining of a different kind.

"Would you consider letting me have the return of my horse in exchange for some dust from Merlin's beard?" Young Henry asked the knight who had just dismounted him at tournament.

"No," the victor replied.

"Ah," Young Henry said, "I see that you care nothing for dust. And yet, sir, you know it is that to which we shall all return."

"That may be, my prince, but as winner of this tournament, I would like something that I can hold in my hands."

"Oh," Young Henry said, "I am relieved to know that, for I was about to offer you the island of England for the return of my horse, but you cannot hold England."

The victorious knight replied, "And neither can the son of King Henry."

The audience gasped. Young Henry frowned, but only for a moment. "Of course, the son of King Henry cannot hold England, for he is as yet unborn. I am the crowned King of England, and I have no son," Young Henry said, "none that my fair wife Marguerite will allow me to admit to."

Everyone laughed, but only two people knew the pain that lay behind that laughter. And only the two of us knew the whole awful truth that was behind the title, "Lord of Little Land."

The jealousy between Richard and Young Henry reached a climax when the brothers met at the Christmas court in the year 1183. Young Henry came, and so did Richard. Geoffrey came, too, and John. John was now seventeen. Richard called John "The Pustule."

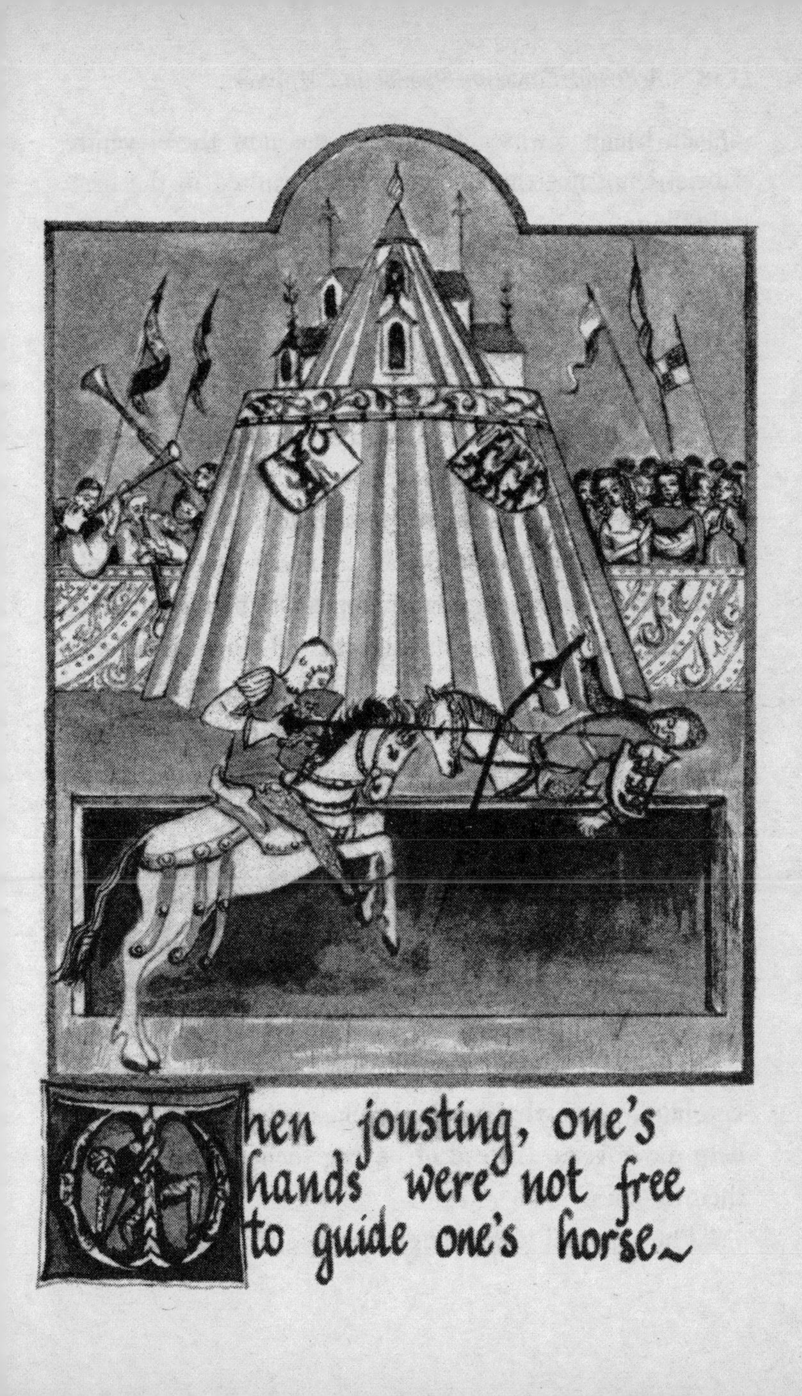
When jousting, one's
hands were not free
to guide one's horse~

Queen Eleanor was not there; it was now the eleventh Christmas since that meeting that resulted in the first rebellion.

When dinner was finished, the family assembled to discuss the business of the realm.

King Henry began. "I am doing great things," he said.

"How modest of you, Father," Richard said.

"Modesty only becomes those who have something to be modest about," the king continued.

"Yes," Richard said, "Father needs only to look around this room to grow immodest. What other king in Europe can brag of having sired three princes and one pustule?"

John stood up and lunged at Richard's throat. Richard quickly grabbed his arms and pinned them behind his back. "Sit," he commanded.

John sat.

The king waited until things were quiet in that part of the room and then he continued. "I *am* doing great things. I am establishing a system of justice throughout England and a system of tax collection that is a model of efficiency. I have gathered together men from all over England, men who speak the Saxon tongue and who help me govern. Instead of paying them in land, I pay them in coin."

"The English are shopkeepers and gardeners at

heart," Richard said. "It is not much of a challenge to govern them. You are welcome to them and to the Normans. I like the men of the Aquitaine; they give me some fight."

Henry replied, "You don't govern, Richard. You thrash about too much to call it that. A man who governs uses his head more than he uses his fist."

"Good for you," King Henry said. "Government is a wonderful occupation, my boys. If ever I climb into Heaven, it will be for what I am doing now." He looked at his oldest son and said, "Henry, why don't you travel to the Aquitaine and help Richard? With your soul and his strength, we Plantagenets can rule an empire greater than Rome."

"I am afraid, sire, that helping Richard will try my soul more than it will save it. Your son Richard is a savage. His genius lies in the number of ways he punishes rebel barons. He not only uproots their orchards, he also sows their fields with salt. But that, too, is not enough; he cuts off the hands and gouges out the eyes of the men he takes captive. His mind is as heavy as his hand; I find that he does nothing new—he only does more."

Richard smiled. He addressed Young Henry. "Tell me, brother, do you believe that there is truth in names?" Young Henry did not answer, and Richard continued, speaking to the room at large. "I, for one, believe there is. For example, someone in this room is called 'Lord of Little Land'; I believe there is truth in that name. I, on the other hand, am called 'Richard the Lion Heart'; I believe there is truth in that name, too."

"Shut up!" Young Henry shouted, his back still turned toward Richard. Richard strode up to his brother, grabbed him by the shoulders and turned him around. Face to face, eye to eye, he said, "A pussy cat does not tell a lion not to roar."

That remark finished forever the conversation between the two brothers. That remark became their declaration of war.

8

I HAD MANY messages to take to Queen Eleanor during the years that the king kept her in Salisbury. Some of my messages were of new losses of old loves: Rosamond Clifford had died. King Louis had, too, and his son Philip Augustus had taken over the French throne. Some of my messages were of the new rebellion, the war between her sons, Richard and Young Henry. The king did all he could to keep his sons from tearing apart the kingdom he had pieced together. He would give aid first to one and then to the other.

Some of my messages were of death.

On Midsummer Day in the year 1183 I arrived at Salisbury. I was told that the queen had set out before sunrise to go to Stonehenge. It had become her custom during her years in prison to watch the midsummer sun rise over the heelstone of that ancient monument. It was hours past sunrise when I arrived at Stonehenge. I found the queen still there, leaning against one of the giant stones and staring at the horizon.

"Good day, my queen," I said.

"It is a bright day, William. Rare for fog-bound

England." She paused a minute and then added, "Your coming has helped me solve a mystery, William."

"The mystery of Stonehenge, madam?"

"No, William. A personal mystery."

"I have some news, my lady," I said.

The queen paid no attention. "The mystery involves a dream I had several nights ago. I dreamed of my son Henry. In my dream I saw him lying still with his hands folded over his chest. On the finger of one hand he wore a blue sapphire ring. The ring cast a pale blue light upward toward his face. But the light shed by the ring was pale compared to the light that flowed downward from his crowns. In my dream, Young Henry was wearing two crowns. One was that which he wore at his coronation, but above that crown of Earthly gold floated another, one that was made more of light than of substance. That dream has troubled me, William. Until now. Now I know the meaning of the dream." Queen Eleanor slowly lifted her eyes and said, "My son Henry is dead, isn't he, William?"

"Yes, my queen, he is."

She sucked in her breath. "He is at rest. The second crown means that he is resting under a Heavenly light. He has found favor with God."

"Yes, my lady."

Queen Eleanor's eyes filled, but she remained composed. "I do not yet understand the meaning of the ring."

"The ring came from his father. It was the king's blue sapphire."

"How did Young Henry come to have his father's ring?"

"A week before he died, Young Henry had come to his father's camp. The two of them came to terms. Young Henry promised that he would meet with Richard and parley for peace. But once outside the king's camp, he fell in once again with those crafty barons who knew how to fan into flames his jealousy of his brother. Instead of parleying for peace, Young Henry attacked the king's men. He came at the king's forces again and again. Waging the war seemed more important than winning it. Then suddenly, Young Henry fell ill. His brow was burning. Light hurt his eyes. The fever was sudden, much like that which men say took his grandfather, Geoffrey the Fair. When Young Henry realized that the fever would consume him, he sent me to his father. I pleaded with the king to come, but he would not. 'My son once promised peace and did not give it. How do I know that this is not a trap?' When I knew that I could not convince the king to come, I asked him for some token that I could take to the young prince. King Henry pulled the sapphire ring from his finger and gave it to me. When I returned to our camp, Young Henry looked more like a spirit than a son of man. He took the ring and put it on his finger. Then he spoke to those of us who were there.

To one of us he gave his boots. He commanded that we take them. To another he gave his cloak; to yet another, his shirt.

"When at last he had disposed of all his worldly goods, even his linen, he smiled at us and said, 'I want to leave this world as plain as I arrived.' Someone said, 'But the ring. You have not removed the ring, my prince.' Young Henry answered, 'I keep that not for want of splendor, but so that when I arrive at Heaven's gate, God shall know that my father has forgiven me. Take it from my finger after my soul departs my body.' Then he smiled and said, 'I shall not wear it long enough for it to tarnish.'

"We tried to remove the ring, but it wouldn't come from his finger. The king has forgiven Young Henry, and the ring shows God his father's forgiveness."

Queen Eleanor was silent for a long time. At last she spoke. "What will the king do now?"

"I do not know, my lady."

She sighed, "I was not asking you, William, as much as I was asking myself. What will you do, William?"

"I shall now serve the father of my former master: your husband, the king."

"Oh, Marshal, I would like you once to know doubt. Not suffer from it, but to know it."

"Why, my lady?"

"Only because I think that a rosy blush adds some interest to true blue and gray chain mail."

9

THE NEXT MESSAGE I brought to Queen Eleanor was a trunk of gifts from the king. She smiled as she unpacked them: a saddle trimmed with gold, two embroidered pillows, and a gown of scarlet, lined with miniver. "Oh, I see that I am to be queen for a day."

King Henry arrived shortly thereafter. It was the first time that they had met since the death of Young Henry. For a moment they were united in sorrow. "He cost me much," the king said. "Would that he could cost me more."

Queen Eleanor replied, "Our son had the head and heart of a king, Henry. Too bad you felt it necessary to keep a king's parts wrapped in a prince's jacket. He was bound to break out."

"Perhaps so, madam. But now we must redistribute our realm. I have a plan."

"I'm sure you do," the queen answered.

"Richard is next in line for the throne," King Henry began.

"Oh, yes, thank you for reminding me, Henry. I was wondering who came next. I was tempted to name our children in alphabetical order so that I would have less trouble remembering."

"Enough of your sarcasm, madam. We have business. As I was saying, Richard is next in line. I want to give him Young Henry's portion, Normandy, Anjou and England."

"What about the Aquitaine, Henry? You are awfully quiet about what you want me to do with the Aquitaine."

"Do you like your new gown, madam?"

"Yes. What about the Aquitaine?"

"Do you like the gold work on your new saddle, madam?"

"Yes. Will the Aquitaine move over one—to Geoffrey?"

"No. Geoffrey can keep Brittany. Do you like the embroidered pillows, madam?"

"Yes. What about the Aquitaine?"

"I'm glad you like your presents, madam. Now that you have brought up the matter of the Aquitaine, madam, I think I ought to tell you that I think we should give it to John."

Queen Eleanor threw back her head and laughed. She roared. "Oh, oh. You'll have to excuse me, Henry, but laughing is what I do instead of losing my temper. I see your plan. Richard is too strong for you. You'll make him Young Henry's heir, all title and no taxes.

And you've pinned all your hopes on John Lackland. I thought you were a better judge of character than that. Shame on you. Richard will never consent to being a phantom king. He has a map of the Aquitaine tattooed in his head. His brain is shaped like its terrain. He cares not a fig for England; he does not even speak the language, and he boasts that he will never learn. You would do better to choose Geoffrey to be your paper king. Yes, Geoffrey is excellent material. He is competent but unimaginative."

"That is enough, madam."

"It is not. Are you blind? Do you not see what John is? You have allowed me no part in his upbringing, and I cannot see that you have done even an average job. You have seen to it that he has been raised without music; you have formed him of mucus and muscle. He either cries for what he wants, or he punches for it. Snot and sinew! There is no bone there to hang a crown on. I will never, never consent to giving the Aquitaine to John."

"Have you quite finished, madam?"

"Yes, I have."

"Well, then, madam, since you seem not to approve of any of our sons, I am taking back all of my lands."

"Do that, Henry, and you will but cause another rebellion."

"The third may be a charm, madam. Perhaps your

sons will make it on their third try. But don't hope for it, madam. It will cost you much."

The queen stood up and said, "I shall not hope for it, Henry. I truly shall not."

10

RICHARD had learned much about rebellion during his years of squashing them in the Aquitaine. He had learned that success in war depends upon help. How many rebellions had he been able to put down just because the nobles foolishly thought that they could fight alone? So Richard wrote to two hundred discontented barons of his father's; he asked for their support, and he got it. He also asked Philip Augustus, the new king of France, for his help, and he got that, too. The two young men, one already a king, and the other wanting to be one, led all the power of France into battle against King Henry.

King Henry was sick; an old leg wound had acted up. He was sick, and he felt old. He was tired. He lost castle after castle. He retreated from the battlefield to nurse his wound, to gather strength. The pain raced from his heel through his legs; he could not walk.

We lost one fortress after another. At last King Henry was summoned by Philip Augustus to parley for peace. King Henry cursed the pain and the fever as he mounted his horse to ride to the place they had agreed upon. The Capet saw how tired King Henry looked, and he offered him a cushion and a cloak on which to rest, but King Henry shook his head. "I have always parleyed astride my horse, and I shall do so even in defeat."

The two kings drew up the terms of the settlement. King Henry had no choice but to agree to what Philip Augustus demanded. He made only one request—that Philip Augustus send him a list of all those barons who had shifted to Richard's side. We were able to ride only a short distance from the place of parley, when King Henry collapsed and had to be carried the rest of the way to his castle at Chinon.

Until the list arrived, the king was full of curses and courage; he was determined to get well, to recover his lost castles, to get revenge. He despised defeat. He despised knowing that the first great defeat he had ever suffered had been the work of one of his sons.

When the list of traitors arrived, the king asked me to read the names to him. I unrolled the parchment and gasped. "Sire, may God help us."

"What is the matter, Marshal?"

"The first name written is that of Count John."

"My son, John Lackland? That same John whom I loved most? That same John for whom I fought this last hateful war?"

I nodded yes.

"Read no more, William," he said. He turned his face to the wall and whispered, "Shame, shame. Shame on a conquered king."

He spoke no more, my king. My one-time foe. My friend.

11

IT WAS now Richard who bade me to cross the Channel to take news of death to the queen. But this time, there was good news, too. I was to set her free.

When I arrived, the queen was giving orders and was very much in charge.

"You know already, my lady?" I asked.

"Of course, I know. Come, William, there is much work to do."

"I am retiring for a while, my queen."

"Retiring, Marshal?"

"I am soon to be something more than a marshal. I am to marry the Duchess of Pembroke. We will live on her estates, and I shall manage them. I shall be an earl. I'll be in Pembroke if you need me."

"I don't know if I shall need you, but Richard will. He is quite a boy, that Richard, that Lion Heart. But he has much to learn. Damn! He's never even learned to speak English. The time he's spent in England since his birth can be measured in weeks. There is much to do to make the people love him."

"He is a direct descendant of King Henry, your

husband, may his soul rest in peace. I know the people will accept him."

"I did not say *accept*, William! I said *love*. I am determined that Richard shall be *loved*. An accepted king accomplishes nothing. A respected king accomplishes something but must fight for what he gets. A loved king has his people fighting for him. Richard will be loved, as I have made King Arthur loved."

"He has a lot to recommend him, my lady. He is handsome. People are always receptive to a comely person. He is a good poet and a chivalrous knight."

"How could any son reared by me in my court at Poitiers not be chivalrous?"

"But Richard is a great knight."

"I see that you have changed sides again, William. Are you now Richard's man?"

"What is strange about that, my lady? I have always been on the side of the Plantagenets."

Queen Eleanor smiled. "Yes, William. You stand firm, and it is we Plantagenets who change partners."

"That is exactly so, my lady. I did not find it difficult to become Richard's man. He is a most chivalrous knight. When I was fighting with King Henry, your husband, may his soul rest in peace, in the battle at Le Mans, I fell behind King Henry, your husband, may his soul . . ."

"Get on with it, William. His soul may rest in peace, but my behind will not. Tell your story straight."

"Yes, my queen. The city of Le Mans was in flames, and I had stopped to help an old lady whose clothing had caught fire. My training as a true and noble knight would not allow me to pass so sad a sight without offering my help."

"Certainly, William."

"Yes. Well, Richard came upon me, and I aimed my lance at him. 'Do not kill me, Marshal,' he said. 'You cannot kill an unarmed man.' And the truth was that Richard wore no armor. The code of chivalry commands that one not fight an unarmed man, so I said, 'May the Devil take you, for I will not.' I then plunged my lance into his horse, for I wanted my king, Henry, your husband, may his . . ."

"William!"

"Yes, my queen. Sorry. I wanted King Henry to be able to escape, and he did. When next I saw Richard, it was at his father's grave. Richard looked at me and said, 'William the Marshal, you tried to kill me the other day.' 'No, sire,' I replied. 'I tried to kill your horse, and I did. I could have thrust my lance in you as easily as I did in your horse. I chose your horse. I cannot believe that I have done wrong.' Richard said, 'I forgive you. I shall not hold it against you.' So you see, my lady, he has forgiveness, and forgiveness is a mark of greatness."

"That may be, William," Queen Eleanor said, "but I must make that mark grow. I am going on a good-will tour, William. I am going to travel to every shire in England and listen to the people. You see, it is always the incidental inconvenience that upsets the common man. I am going to right some incidental wrongs. And that is the first thing that I am going to do to make Richard the Lion Heart a great king. The English will claim him for theirs, and they will love him, even if he can't speak their language. He ought to learn it though, William. English is a strong language. It has a great assortment of four-lettered words."

Back
in
Heaven

ELEANOR SMILED at William the Marshal, at Matilda-Empress and at Abbot Suger. "I was sixty-seven when I was let out of prison. I believe that my real life began then. I had used that time. I had lost two husbands and two sons before I was released, for Geoffrey had died, too, of the fever that plagued the Plantagenets. Yet for all those losses, I felt that I had gained something while I was there."

"What could you have gained in prison?"

"Understanding," Eleanor answered. "Understanding freedom for one thing. It looks even brighter when viewed from its dark side. As a matter of fact, when I arrived Up, and I was asked what age I wanted to be, I answered *sixty-seven* without a moment's hesitation. And I answered, knowing that I would be sixty-seven for all Eternity. I could have chosen twenty-five when I was fresh and comely in Constantinople, and I could have chosen thirty when I was madly in love with Henry, but I chose sixty-seven. For I wanted all those years, even the years in prison, with me in Heaven."

Matilda-Empress said, "One thing you never learned in prison was to slow down your tongue."

"But something has softened it," Abbot Suger commented.

"Don't defend me, dear Suger," Eleanor said, laughing. "Move over, all of you. It's time I told about myself. From this point on, no one can speak for me. Being in prison is like looking at life inside out. You learn to know its fabric and its seams. After I was released from prison, I learned what it means to be a queen."

"I never knew you to have any doubts about that," Matilda-Empress said.

"Then say that I learned not *to know* but *to understand*."

"Excuse me for interrupting, Queen Eleanor, but it is soon the time for King Henry's verdict."

"The noble knight still does not forget a purpose." She looked over the three of them and laughed. "All right. All of you are more interested in the gossip of my life than in its spirit. Even you, Abbot. Now, listen while I take you rapidly through the last fifteen years of my life. Listen, all of you, while I push you into the thirteenth century."

Part Four

1

I TRAVELED throughout England after Henry's death, and as I did, I made friends. For one thing, I relieved the monks of the chore of keeping Henry's horses. Henry had demanded that he have fresh relays of horses throughout his territories, and he had forced the abbeys to maintain his stables. They resented that; I excused them from the responsibility, and I did so in Richard's name; that made the monks very happy.

Then I began a uniform system of weights and measures for the whole country. What an aggravation to have a piece of cloth measured by one system in Nottingham and by an entirely different system in Oxford. That made the merchants very happy.

And I did the same for coins. I made a uniform system of coins to be used throughout the country. That made everyone but the money changers very happy. It benefited no one but the money changers for a merchant traveling from the city of Sandwich to have to change money at the borders of Canterbury, a few miles away. And to show that Richard was responsible, I had his face engraved on the coins.

And everywhere I went, I listened to the people, and I served justice. In castle after castle, I set free all those poor souls who were waiting for Henry to finish his wars with his sons so that he could hold court. In his last years Henry had become a fanatic about people who hunted on his royal grounds. Henry would kill a man for killing a deer. I stopped that, too.

And I did all this in Richard's name.

For entertainment I planned Richard's coronation. The people of England were entitled to a festival, and they had it. There is nothing like a lavish display to give people pride in their country. Governments still do it; they call them *World Fairs* or *Inaugurations*, but they are what a coronation was—an acceptable form of showing off.

By the time Richard arrived on the shores of England, he was everyone's hero. Right after his coronation, he announced his desire to go on Crusade to Jerusalem. The Holy City had finally been captured by the Turks, and Richard thought it was time for a Plantagenet to take the cross. King Philip Augustus was to go, too, and so was Frederick Barbarossa, King of Germany. My son with the sons of the two kings who had led the Second Crusade, the Crusade that I and my Amazons had gone on.

Richard was outfitted according to his tastes and mine; both of us shared a love of splendor. Philip Augustus was no match for Richard the Lion Heart.

He was not handsome, and he had only one eye that worked. Richard was richer, handsomer, and more popular. Philip was jealous.

Shortly after the men started their journey, I made a journey, too. I went to Spain, and there I fetched a princess. I took her to Sicily where Richard was waiting for some ships that would carry him to the Holy Land. Richard liked my choice, and so he married the princess.

I had to do that. Richard had no heir, and if he should die on Crusade, I wanted someone other than my son John to claim the throne.

The Third Great Crusade ended with the following results: Frederick Barbarossa drowned. Philip Augustus got sick and lost all his hair, his fingernails and toenails, and he was less than handsome to begin with. After he lost those parts, Philip Augustus went home—before the real fighting began. Richard was shipwrecked on his way home and was captured in Austria and held for a king's ransom; it took me two years to raise the money to set him free.

While Richard was prisoner, Philip began attacking our castles in the Vexin. Before they had left for the Crusade, Philip had asked for the return of the Vexin. He had argued that since Young Henry was dead and Marguerite had returned to the Capets, the Vexin should, too. The Vexin had been given to us only as her dowry. Richard had stalled him. "Let us settle these differences after the Crusade," he had said. "Let us not talk of distributing the Earth. Let us first save it. For Christianity."

Philip Augustus was not the man that his father was. Louis would never have broken the Truce of God; he would never have attacked another man's castles—especially when that man had been captured fighting a battle that he had run out on.

Richard returned at last as a conquering hero. Even though Jerusalem was still in the hands of the Turks, he had made a treaty that would allow Christians to visit the Holy City. Philip was more jealous than ever of Richard's popularity and reputation. And the fighting over the Vexin got more serious.

It was not in any great battle that Richard met that arrow. It was not in any important siege that my son met death, and it was not any famous warrior who fired the arrow that killed him. Richard's death was brutal and painful. And meaningless. But I must tell of it to show that my son Richard earned his name, Lion Heart.

A young man, not an important young man, was defending the walls of a castle, not an important castle, that was under siege by Richard's men. The young man used a fry-pan for a shield, and he used as weapons the arrows he could pull from the castle walls, those very arrows which Richard's men had fired at him. The young man fired at a mounted knight, and the arrow pierced the knight's shoulder, and it went deep. The boy did not know that he had felled a king.

No one, except the men immediately near him, knew that Richard was hurt. Richard finished his round of inspection and went to his tent and there, at last, he allowed the men to pull the arrow from his shoulder, but it had gone deep, too deep. As the men pulled, the shaft broke. The men gouged at Richard's flesh in an attempt to cut the barb out. They plunged searching fingers into the raw meat of my son's shoulder, but their fingers could not pry loose that sharp triangle of iron. It stayed to rust, to rot. Richard knew he would not live. He asked to have the young man who fired the arrow brought before him.

"Why," asked Richard of the scared young man, "why did you wish to injure me?"

"Because," the boy said, "you killed my father and my brother. I do not repent. Do with me as you like."

"Go in peace," Richard said. "I forgive you for my death." The Lion Heart commanded that the boy be unchained. Then he died.

Richard died. He was forty-two years old; he had no son. I would now have to construct a king out of John Lackland.

2

THERE WAS MUCH to be done. I was seventy-seven years old, and I did not know if I would have enough years to do something with John. That spoiled, reckless John.

The narrow slits of prison walls had sharpened my focus on my times. I realized that there was rising a new class of people, something between noble and peasant, a middle class. They were merchants, they had money, and they would be heard. So as I rode through the towns of my native lands, my Aquitaine, I granted charters to these towns. The people then became responsible for their own government—and for their own defense. I knew that I could not expect these people to be loyal to John. But, I could expect them to take pride in a town they could call their own, and I gave them their freedom. For a price.

I also visited abbeys and made arrangements for my body to rest in Fontevrault next to Henry's and Richard's. Of course I chose Fontevrault; it was the only abbey in all of France that housed both nuns and monks, but which had a nun not a monk as its head.

I established hospitals, another important good work

The people of Poitiers receive the charter for their town from Eleanor of Aquitaine.

that makes one popular. And I saw to it that the roads were in good order; the merchant class needed to transport their goods, and I needed them on my side.

And then to insure peace, I went to King Philip Augustus and there in front of all the court of Paris, I swallowed my pride, bent my rusty knees and paid homage to a Capet. A gentle reminder that I wanted peace; I was reminding Philip that he was my overlord and was sworn to protect me. Me and mine. John was mine.

3

THE QUESTION of the Vexin was still not settled. It was, as it had been, on and off for forty years, a raw sore between the lands of the Capets and the Plantagenets. I had a plan for that, too. I thought it would be a good idea if Philip's son became engaged to one of my granddaughters. The Vexin, which we still held, could then go to Philip's son as dowry for my granddaughter. What a strange fate for that land. That same Vexin that had brought Henry to the court of King Louis and that Louis had traded back in exchange for the marriage of their Marguerite to our Young Henry would now be the parcel of trade for the marriage of one grandson of King Louis for one granddaughter of mine.

At that time I had outlived all my children but two: John, who was King of England, and Eleanor, who was Queen of Castile. The daughter who was my namesake had lived in Spain since she was in her early teens.

And so it was that at the age of eighty, I crossed the mountains between France and Spain in the middle of winter. I arrived to fetch a granddaughter of mine as a bride for a grandson of my ex-husband. I found my daughter Eleanor worthy of my name. Her court was gay and beautiful, and so was she. My daughter Eleanor had eleven children, one more than I had had, and it had taken me two husbands to do it.

Of Eleanor's eleven children, two girls were eligible to be wives for Philip's son. They paraded the girls before me, and the girls bowed and curtsied and performed. It was expected that I choose the elder, the one named Urraca.

We were at the table, and the two girls were sitting on either side of me. Both of them had manners that were tidy and serene. "What do you like best to do?" I asked them.

Urraca, the elder, answered, "There is nothing I like better than the songs of the troubadours. I love to listen to the troubadours."

"And you?" I asked Blanca, the younger of the two.

Blanca answered, "I like to read, and I like to ride. Both reading and riding allow me to go as far and as deep as I choose."

I picked Blanca as the future queen of France. When my daughter asked why, I told her, "The French could never like someone with as foreign a name as Urraca. We'll make Blanche out of Blanca, and the French will love her."

And so I marched back over the mountains to France with my bounty, Blanca, Blanche of Castile. I was delighted. I was still enough of a judge of people to know that a girl who wants control over her spare time can control a kingdom. Time proved my judgment to be correct.

There was peace in England and France when I died. I did not die without cares, but I did die without regrets.

My life was marked by good happenings, bad happenings and sad ones, too. There were times when the bad and the sad could have weighed me down. But to drink life from only the good is to taste only half of it. When I died in that year 1204, I smiled, knowing that I had drunk fully of both flavors. I had wasted nothing.

Back
in
Heaven

"HOW DID YOU feel when you learned that your son King John is considered the worst king that England has ever had?" Abbot Suger asked.

"I am not too impressed with such ratings," Eleanor replied. "John was spoiled and fickle, but he had wit and fits of generosity. After Richard died, I got to know him better. I was only sorry that I didn't have more time to develop his better nature."

"How did you feel when you learned that the barons made him sign the great charter, the Magna Carta, at Runnymede?"

"I was annoyed."

"Where is Young Henry?" Matilda-Empress asked. "He should be here to greet his father."

William the Marshal cleared his throat. "Young Henry sent me in his stead."

"I see that even in Heaven my grandson needs a marshal," Matilda-Empress said. She then turned to Eleanor and asked, "What did you mean when you said that time has proven you correct about Blanche of Castile? Blanche has a reputation for being the worst mother-in-law in all of history. She hasn't even come Up yet."

Eleanor answered, "She was bad as a mother-in-law, but as a queen she did very well. When her husband died, she held the kingdom together until her son was ready to take over."

Matilda-Empress said, "*I* did as much."

"As much, perhaps, but not as well. There was the episode of Stephen, your worthless nephew, as you have referred to him."

"But I did raise my son to be a great king."

"And Blanche of Castile raised hers to be a great king and a saint. My great-grandson was King Louis IX who became Saint Louis, the only French king to become a saint."

"Well!" Matilda-Empress exclaimed. "Your sainted great-grandson is my sainted great-great-grandson. I am great-great-grandmother to a saint. And you are great-grandmother to the same one." She paused a minute and smiled at Eleanor. "Abbot Bernard of Clairvaux would never have believed it."

"Not during his lifetime," Eleanor agreed, "but in Heaven all things are possible . . . even. . . ." Eleanor's voice faded as she looked in the distance.

Abbot Suger, Matilda-Empress, and William the Marshal also looked. They saw three men coming toward them: one on the left, tall and gaunt, wearing a

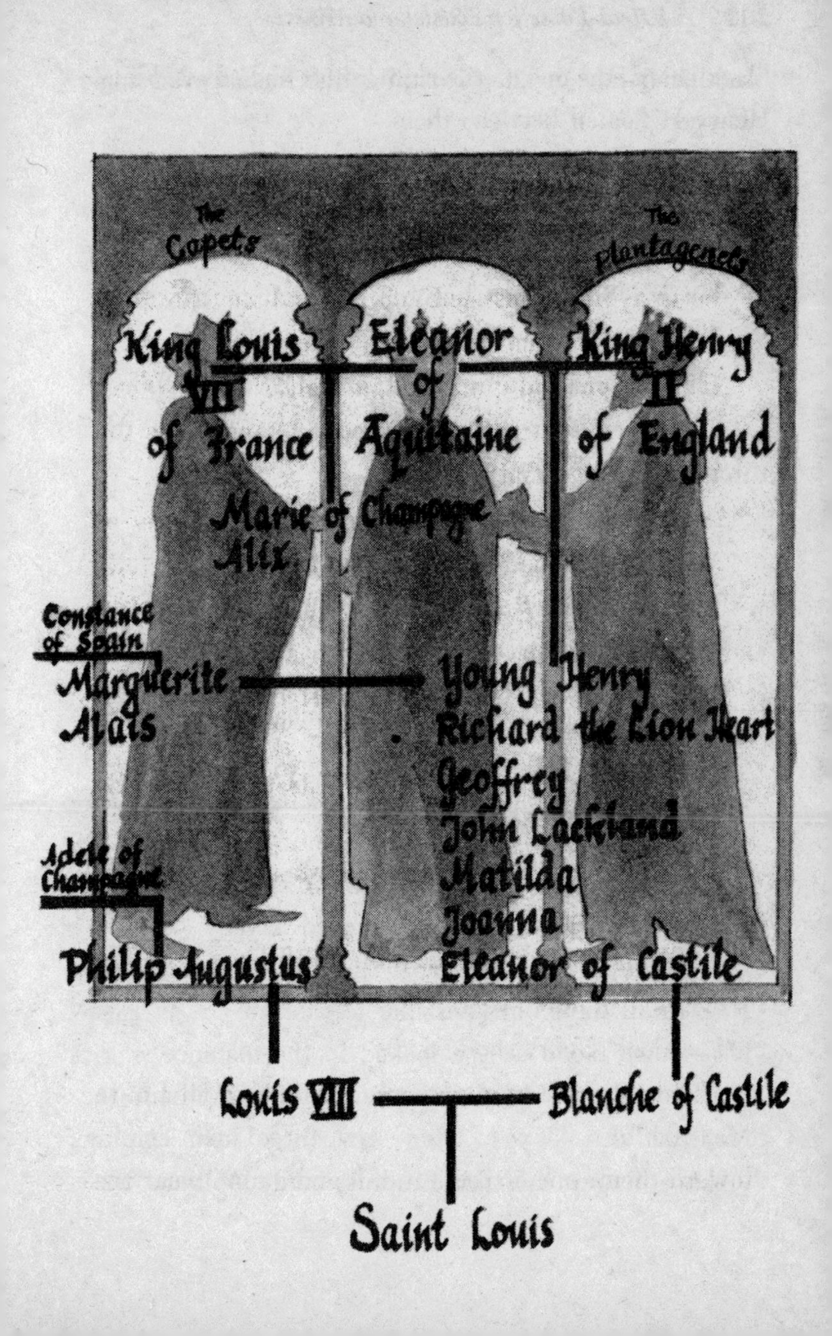
The Capets
The Plantagenets
King Louis VII of France
Eleanor of Aquitaine
King Henry II of England
Marie of Champagne
Alix
Constance of Spain
Marguerite
Alais
Young Henry
Richard the Lion Heart
Geoffrey
John Lackland
Matilda
Joanna
Eleanor of Castile
Adele of Champagne
Philip Augustus
Louis VIII
Blanche of Castile
Saint Louis

black beard, the one on the right, short and squat. King Henry II floated between them.

Henry took his first look at Eleanor in eight hundred years. He looked her over from toe to brow. Then he spoke, "Good grief, madam! One of these men says that he is a Mr. Winston Churchill and that he governed England. How can a common man govern?"

"This one did quite well, actually," Eleanor replied.

"You mean that a common man now sits on the throne of England?"

"No, Henry. A rather plain housewife does."

"And this one," Henry said, pointing to the tall man with the beard, "says that he is a Mr. Abraham Lincoln and that he is an American lawyer and president. What is a president? And what in Heaven's name is an American?"

"In Heaven's name, Henry?" Eleanor asked. "Everything here is in Heaven's name."

"Now, madam," Henry said, "don't act *holier than thou* with me."

"But I am *holier than thou*, Henry. I have been Up for over five hundred years."

"Eleanor!" Henry shouted.

"Sh, sh, sh," Eleanor answered. "There's a lot I have to tell you."

Abbot Suger, Matilda-Empress and William the

Marshal floated away. The Messrs. Churchill and Lincoln left, too.

Then at last King Henry II of England and his wife, Eleanor of Aquitaine, were left alone in a corner of Heaven to catch up with eight hundred years of history.

But they will.

They have all Eternity to do it.